Flesh
Wound

❖❖

Flesh
Wound

❖❖

Paul
Grescoe

Douglas & McIntyre
Vancouver/Toronto

❖❖

Douglas & McIntyre Ltd.
1615 Venables Street
Vancouver, British Columbia V5L 2H1

Canadian Cataloguing in Publication Data
Grescoe, Paul, 1939-
Flesh wound
ISBN 0-88894-731-3
I. Title. PS8563.R48F4 1991   C813'.54   C91-091318-8
PR9199.3.G74P4 1991

All the characters and events in *Flesh Wound* are entirely fictional. Any resemblance they may bear to real persons and experiences is illusory.

Design by Robert MacDonald/MediaClones
Cover design and illustration by Alexandra Hass
Printed and bound in Canada by D. W. Friesen & Sons Ltd.
Printed on acid-free paper

For Audrey

1

Shoot

❖❖

The waiting is always the worst. Waiting for the subject, wondering when he'll show. If he will. Worrying this time that he had spotted me in my Austin Mini and wouldn't leave the refuge of his house halfway down the block. Tense, I was burbling wordless little tunes. My whole world had become the 250 feet fronting the wide white-stucco house with the red-tiled roof.

The mansions along Southwest Marine run to Pseudo Spanish Colonial and Fake French Regency. They rise behind big red cedars, set in expensive acres of lovingly tended land which slants down to the delta of the Fraser. Nice as the neighbourhood was, I couldn't let my eyes stray for more than a few moments. An early April sun was toasting the left half of my face. My spine felt as if it had parted in several places. My bladder was setting a new Canadian record for fluid retention.

Occasionally a thick lump of cars would clot the steady stream of university traffic that made the road all but impassable for pedestrians. A long-limbed teenager in private-school tartan skirt hesitated on the sidewalk ahead. Her arms burdened with books, she looked for an opening. After a couple of false starts, she loped across the pavement. Her thoroughbred legs had taken her halfway over when a book fell. *Don't stop!* But she stopped to scoop it up, just long enough to present easy pickings for an oncoming sportscar. Brakes squalled. The car fishtailed. As it shuddered to a rest on the shoulder, the girl bolted around it and down a driveway, disappearing through the pillared doorway of her house.

My body was suddenly chill. I shook my head, trying to scatter the memories. Was that how it had happened for Sarah, all those years ago? Had she paused for an instant as she crossed the road? Did she see the car as it flung itself at her? Witnesses said it had never even slowed as it struck Sarah and hurled her suddenly limp form on the sidewalk. Its driver had not even stopped to see that she lay there dead.

Enough.

I watched the driver of the sportscar trying to wedge himself back on to Southwest Marine. Nothing like a little street theatre to heighten the tension. By now I had been waiting seven and a half hours. About ten-thirty I'd finished the three pork-and-dill-pickle sandwiches I was saving for lunch. At noon, just as k.d. lang was twanging through "Three Cigarettes in the Ashtray" on my tapedeck, I'd run out of Craven "A"s. Worried that the car's battery was ebbing as fast as mine was, I'd turned off the tape. And by one I had glanced so often at the front page of a day-old *Vancouver Sun* that I could pass a Master's defence on all three columns of the feature story.

It was an interesting story, the first hour I'd read it. The headline hollered:

Police have 'no leads'
in Wreck Beach slaying
of Hollywood starlet

Young and sexy Bobbi Flynn had been murdered in Vancouver, where she'd been making a movie called *The Empty Gun*. One suddenly mild morning ten days ago, a six-year-old came across her nude body face down on Wreck Beach. The fact that the redheaded lady had no clothes on probably didn't bother the boy because he had none on either. He and his folks were sunbathing in the buff just below the UBC campus. The beach is a skinny stretch of sand littered with artfully arranged boulders and driftwood logs. Weekend nudists love its privacy: to get there you have to be deranged enough to clamber down a rotting cliff. I used to lie around there myself, posing like a page out of *Sunshine and Health*. But that was ten years ago, when I was twenty-five and could still suck in my stomach without rupturing myself.

Apparently Bobbi Flynn had a nice lean stomach. I remembered seeing a review of her first movie in *Maclean's* a year before. Canada's Weekly Newsmagazine said that while she certainly couldn't act, her long slinky body had all the kick of a martini before lunch. Now it had been shaken, not stirred, and served on the rocks. With a twist: the wicked blue marks they found around her neck weren't made by a diamond choker. A friend at the *Sun* told me that Bobbi's butchered corpse had looked like the work of a lunatic. Where her roseate breasts had been, there were now carmine patches of blood and gristle.

The slam of a door suspended my reverie.

My man was hobbling down his driveway. Finally. Forty-five, fat, bulging out of his black pinstripe, he was hunched over as if in pain. Looking left and right, he walked slowly, cautiously to his Mercedes. I tensed, waiting for the moment. He got in the car and turned on the ignition. Not yet. The car waited for a hole in the traffic, then accelerated on to Southwest Marine. Heading towards me, it had a definite list to the right and began to sound like a helicopter chopping the air. Stop, dammit.

❖❖

It stopped, veering on to the shoulder a hundred yards from my car, where I slouched hidden behind the steering wheel. Perfect.

The fat man got out of the Mercedes and looked at the front tire on the driver's side. Flat. Of course. I'd let most of the air out five hours ago. He kicked the tire in anger and then strode to the trunk, opened it and wrestled out a jack and tire iron.

Soon. I picked up the motor-driven Nikon, raised it to eye level and, leaning out my open window, aimed it at the Mercedes' front tire. It was easily within range.

Any moment. Fats, presumably no longer in agony, had pried off the hubcap. Now he was yanking the tire iron, desperately trying to loosen the nuts I'd over-tightened early that morning. His bulk was framed beautifully in the lens.

Now.

"Okay, Rudnicki, what the hell ya think you're doing?" A hand with knuckles the size of walnuts grabbed my left arm and twisted it at an unusual angle down the side of the car door. I yelped.

"Get outta the car, snoop."

It was Wylie, a uniform cop. *Holera!* —as my father always said in Ukrainian when he smacked his thumb with a hammer. I noticed that the fat man down the road, spotting this little street drama, had dropped the tire iron and was hurriedly limping, not striding, back to his house.

"Let's see your licence, Rudnicki," Wylie demanded as I unfolded from the Mini. He stood about six-two, or seven inches higher than me. With my one remaining arm, I found my wallet in the jacket of my rumpled cord suit and showed Wylie my licence: Danylo Rudnicki of TransWorld Security, registered under the British Columbia Private Investigators and Security Agencies Act. Actually, I answer to Dan Rudnicki. I don't let anybody but my father call me Danylo. I'll never forgive my mother, God rest her chauvinistic Ukrainian soul.

"Not that licence, dick. Your driver's licence." Wylie was not a chum. Nor were any of his brother officers on the Vancouver force my pals. Not since they'd learned I neglected to tip them off that a woman friend of mine with the *Sun* was going to write an exposé about their after-hours club. One evening, with the help of a photographer, Nadia had looked in on the cops as they whiled away their leisure time on the roof of a downtown building. They tended to drink a lot there in summer and disport themselves with well-known prostitutes. After her story appeared, four drug-squad detectives were suspended without pay for three months. Unfortunately the internal-investigation officers handling the case heard that one of the ladies scheduled for that evening's rooftop performance had been warned off by an acquaintance who worked for a security company. Me.

Wylie would not let bygones go by. "Who're ya hassling now, Rudnicki," he said, snatching my driver's licence. "Some poor widow woman who can't afford to pay her phone bill?"

"No, some stinking rich stockbroker who's lying to his insurance company that he can't bend over since his accident."

"Your left tail-light's broken," Wylie bantered. "And your rear licence plate is completely obscured by dirt. You're getting tickets for both those, *Danylo.*" His junior partner at the wheel of the blue-and-white behind us was smirking under his precisely manicured mustache. "Oh, and let's see that fancy camera of yours." Wylie took it from the seat of the car with exaggerated care and examined the thing as if it were about to explode. Handing it back, he dropped the $800 Nikon FM2, lens down, on to the pavement. "I'm *sorry*, Mr. Rudnicki," he said.

Shit! —as I always said when somebody smashed my boss's brand-new camera.

❖❖

❖❖

Driving home, I wondered—not for the first time—what Dan Rudnicki, political-science major, single father, nice guy, was doing working for a Canadian branch plant of an American security firm. Specialists in insurance claims and white-collar crime and not above doing some slimy industrial spying on the side. Maybe I was simply stupid.

I would take comfort in that theory in days to come. It would help explain why I'd go freelance and get too involved in trying to figure who killed a Hollywood starlet named Bobbi Flynn.

2

The Setup

❖❖

The phone rang at eight the next morning. I let it ring, trying to convince myself that my allergy was really a sneak attack of the flu. It was allergy. I picked up the phone.

"Dan Rudnicki?" a woman's voice wondered.

"Mmm."

"This is Mr. Adam Graves' secretary. He's wondering when you're going to make it to the studio." The voice was laid-back Los Angeles, casual yet quite unapproachable.

Graves? Studio? Oh sure. Graves, I vaguely remembered from the *Sun* story, was executive producer of *The Empty Gun*. The L.A. lady assumed I knew who her boss was. When she heard nothing but the noisy rattle of my clogged sinuses, she offered: "The people at TransWorld Security gave us your number and said you'd be here for the first shoot at seven this morning . . . Are you usually so silent?"

"Usually." The only investigator's trick that works consistently is to shut your mouth and let the other guy reluctantly enliven the dead air. In this case I was merely groping for time. Maybe my boss had left a message about this job on my answering machine, which I hadn't bothered to check last night.

My silence was split by a sudden shriek behind me.

"Hold on," I told the secretary and bounded to the hallway. The shriek had turned into a loud wailing. Esther. "Larissa, what the hell are you doing to Esther?"

"Absolutely nothing. It was *her*, father."

"Liar!"

Esther is a soft little eleven-year-old and her sister, Larissa, is a large, clever thirteen-year-old. Sarah and I had screwed up with the girls' names. We democratically named the first one Larissa because I'm Ukrainian and the second Esther because Sarah was Jewish. Except Larissa is dark and Judaic like her mother while Esther is blonde and bohunk like the old man. Despite their addled genealogy, they both ate my father's borsch and my mother-in-law's blintzes indiscriminately.

"Behave, or I won't take you to the Bryan Adams concert tonight," I threatened, playing my highest card.

"I'm back," I told the L.A. lady on the phone. "Sorry about the delay in getting there. I was on a stakeout all night and just got in a few minutes ago." The lie came too easily, as usual. "I'll be at the studio within the hour."

She sounded relieved, if a little unsettled. "Do you know Cypress Studios in West Vancouver?"

"In an hour." Hanging up, I noticed the flashing light on my AnswerPhone. Jimmy had delivered the message in the growl he passed off as a voice. I knew most of it: there was a job at Cypress, be there at seven, the head guy's name is Adam Graves. "Oh yeah, and it has something to do with that Bobbi Flynn murder. This might be more than straight security work, Rudnicki, so look alive."

I dressed, downed an orange juice with a raw egg, built a coffee, and eased out to the balcony off the kitchen where the tyrannical Larissa wouldn't see me sneaking a contraband cigarette. Human again, I told the girls to get to school, to remember their lunches—and I still wanted a kiss even though I'd yelled at them.

The municipality of West Vancouver, sprawling like some high-class courtesan on the flanks of the North Shore mountains, looks down on Vancouver. The waters of Burrard Inlet separate it from the city's deepsea docks and office towers, from all the unseemly sweat and grime. The three-lane Lion's Gate bridge that grudgingly links the two centres was built during the Depression by the Guinness brewing family of Britain. The Guinnesses found themselves with property to develop on the North Shore and then had to coax the colonials to put up pricey homes on the land by giving them a bridge to get back into Vancouver to earn all the money they needed to support their expensive housing habits. Half a century later the burghers of West Van are still paying off their palaces and clogging the Lion's Gate with their Volvos and BMWs. The town is simply getting too big for its bridges.

This morning I didn't care. The drive up to the studio in my fading '76 Austin Mini 1000 was soothingly slow. The sunroof was open. A sweet wind off the Pacific had carried the pollution over the coastal mountains and left behind a surrealistic blue sky. It was calming to think that I'd called in sick. That I wouldn't be spending the day in the men's wear department of The Bay, posing as a salesman to see who on the staff was stealing the pants off the store.

Cypress Studios slouched across an evergreen plateau below Hollyburn Mountain. There was no guard at the studio gate. There was no gate, just an opening in the spruce trees for a long slalom of a driveway that led me to a hangar-sized sound stage. Outside, amid a snake-pit of cables, stood the false front of a tacky pawnbroker's storefront. Hearing noises and voices behind a tall sliding door, I invited myself in to the world of movie magic.

A few dozen people—stagehands in jeans and message T-shirts, extras in wintry streetclothes costumes—were milling around a two-storey set. It was a cutaway interior of what looked like a skid-road roominghouse. Men wearing earphones looked down from catwalks as a crane rose to the top floor of the house. A round little man with a full ebony beard sat behind a camera on the crane. "Fine," he barked through a loudhailer, "let's rehearse this." Two actors costumed as gun-wielding American cops skulked up a flight of roominghouse stairs. "Fine, fine," the man at the camera murmured through the bullhorn in a muted English accent. "That's it . . . wait at the door . . . Fine. Now we'll do a take. Oh, shit. Where the devil is Cowan?" he said as the crane lowered him to the floor.

He sank into a folding chair with the name Robert Melts stenciled on the back. Melts was the director, I recalled from the *Sun* article, a transplanted Londoner living in Montreal long enough to be considered Canadian. And Canadians were only too eager to claim him. "Someone get that damnable Cowan out of his dressing room," he shouted.

Peter Cowan. The star of *The Empty Gun.* He'd long ago traded the insecurity of the Toronto stage for silk-and-money success on a Hollywood screen. Occasionally he would come back home to do domestic movies that demanded a Canadian-born lead who had proved himself a certified star because he'd made it anywhere else but Canada.

"If Cowan is not on this set within two minutes, tell him that he needn't bother to appear at all," Robert Melts called after the retreating back of a woman running to find the star. In hope of hunting down Adam Graves, I followed her outside. Around the pawnshop flat, where I stumbled over the lighting cables. Through a door at the far end of the building. And into an outer office decorated with an overdressed redhead of a secretary and posters of movies I'd never heard of. Tax-shelter movies.

As the breathless woman arrived, Peter Cowan was leaving. *Exiting left.*

He looked larger than his six-foot-one, beefy, his once-chiselled jaw sagging into a second chin, and the familiar slabs of sideburns turning to white velvet. "Of course we're terrified," Cowan was intoning to the man beside him. "This is frightening."

His audience was about five years younger than Cowan's fifty or so, half a head shorter and, although a little puffy, as delicately built as Cowan was big. He patted the star on his shoulder and said in a tenor voice trying hard to be a baritone: "For crissake, Peter, don't worry. I'm getting my own people on it today. These Canadian cops are looking up their keisters."

"Mr. Melts needs you . . . now, if possible, Mr. Cowan," the panicky messenger woman said.

"The old hack has finally figured out how the hell to shoot that scene, has he?" I detected a certain disrespect in his voice. It might be the only detection I'd do today.

The upholstered secretary with the long face acknowledged my presence. "Can I help you?" she asked in her well-chilled L.A. accent. Violet-ringed eyes squinted from behind random strands of her dye-job hair, making her look like a mournful Irish setter.

"Rudnicki."

"Oh, Mr. Graves"—she turned to the man ushering Cowan out the door—"here's the, uh, detective."

Graves was obviously taken aback too. He was no Gulliver in Lilliput, but he did manage a couple of inches on me. I guessed that I wouldn't be getting the role of Cowan's double in *The Empty Gun.*

"You're Ru—"

"Rudnicki." Rude, with the stress on the nick.

"Rinicky. C'mon in. You're late. But I hear you were on a stakeout all night. You catch the guy?"

Sitting down, he was almost swallowed whole by a wing-backed brown leather chair. It blended well with the walnut desk, which was about as broad as a billiard table, and with the walnut panelling of the impress-the-peons office.

"Oh, we got him cold. On camera. And the cops were right there on the scene. May I sit?"

"Yeah. Sit."

As I parked in a heavy-looking leather chair, it skittered backwards and I wound up poised on the edge like a fright-ened kid in the principal's office. Casters.

Graves was on hold. He seemed impatient to shift from the ping-pong of social nicety to the hardball of business. I let the silence linger, taking the time to catalogue him. Slight nose, small blue eyes, a patch of pimples on his puffball of a face, full head of crinkly brown hair, about a three o'clock shadow. He was garbed in Beverly Hills basic: chunky gold bracelet, slim gold watch, diamond-studded gold ring, white sneakers, white linen pants, and a pale blue linen shirt designed to be worn open to the navel but which he kept buttoned to the neck. Maybe all his gold chains were in for appraisal.

"So. You know about our problem. Our mess. Bobbi's getting killed was a disaster. I mean, everybody's upset about losing her. Of course. She could've been big. But what I called you people about—it's making mincemeat out of our sched-ule. And it's scaring away the investors. We're trying to raise another four and a half million to finish the picture. It's costing us bucks. *Mega*-bucks."

"Can't you replace Bobbi Flynn?"

"Kid, that's not the problem. She had only one scene left to shoot and we can write it out of the picture . . . You want a splash?" A bottle of Remy Martin cognac, near death, perched on a stack of scripts. I declined. He drained the bottle into a snifter. I lit up a Craven "A". "The problem is that the cops

18

haven't one lousy idea about who killed her, and my people are getting paranoid that there's some wacko running around loose in the studio."

"The police have anything?" I knew the answer.

"Nothing. They've spent days interviewing every-goddam-body in the place and found—*zero*. Zip. Which is where you come in. I don't know how terrific a detective you are, kiddo. I don't give a damn. What I need you for is to hang around asking questions for the next few days, let everybody know you're supposed to be investigating Bobbi's dying on us."

So that was it. "You want me to go through the motions?" My first real detecting and I have to play-act. I should have finished my thesis on "The Role of the Foreign Investment Review Act In Restricting Japanese Multinationals in Canada" and become a high-school history teacher.

"I didn't say that. If you get lucky—wonderful. And listen, this is important: I can even give you a lead you can follow up. The cops sure as hell won't. Those bastards put me through the hoops. As if I did it."

"Where were you when it happened?"

"I was coming to that. Don't interrupt."

I filed that away for future deference. "Next time I'll raise my hand and ask permission."

He ignored my sally. "I was damn lucky I was with someone that night. Someone? Hell, she was a hooker. But it turned out one of the cops knew her and found her and they believed she was with me at the right time."

My bushy blond eyebrows lifted.

"Listen, I don't have to pay for it, friend. There was a damn good reason for that whore to be at my place. Bobbi—well, you're going to find out so you'd better hear it from me. Bobbi went both ways." By now my eyebrows were almost brushing my long unruly forelock. "Yeah, she was a bi. A bisexual. And she was screwing the hooker. *And* the picture."

"Why the picture?"

❖❖

Graves held up one hand like a traffic warden. "I've got to take a quick leak. The booze. I'll be back in a minute."

"I could use the john too. Coffee. Is there room enough for both of us?"

"Sure," he sighed. We took a side door out of his office that led to a hallway and the men's washroom, with its toilet compartment and three urinals.

"Be my guest," I said, waving him ahead of me.

"Nah, go ahead. I'll use the toilet." As we relieved ourselves of the morning's liquids, Graves resumed our interrupted conversation. "Why was Bobbi screwing the picture? Melts—Bob Melts, the director—had a thing for her. He has a *thing* for every sweet-assed piece who ever works on his pictures. Anyway, he finds out that Bobbi and the hooker are humping every night and then the next morning Bobbi's all cute and cockteasing, promising Melts that she'll be making it with him that night—"

"And she never does."

"And she never did. So this night I have the hooker come over to my place in West Vancouver to have a talk with her and tell her to lay off Bobbi, I'll even pay her to stay away so maybe Melts will stop throwing tantrums on the set and Bobbi will stop locking herself up in the dressing room. The hooker bought it. It took me five hours of being nice and then yelling and screaming at her—and those five hours happened to be during the time the autopsy boys decided that Bobbi died. Anyway, I paid the whore off and the next day after they found the body, the cops talked to her and she established my alibi. Otherwise I would've been on the roof."

"On the what?"

"I would've been in deep trouble. Anyway, that's the lead I was telling you about."

I'd finished, rinsed my hands and for the last couple of minutes was waiting for him like a patient Daddy. He'd obviously finished too—I couldn't hear him tinkle. Shake it more than three times, Graves, and you're playing with yourself. Finally, I heard him pull up his pants, zip up and flush the toilet. He emerged, washed up and led me back to his office. Where he downed his two inches of cognac in a single swallow. I grimaced for him.

"Okay," he said. "The lead I've got for you. I figure that the hooker might know something, maybe something important—I mean, she was screwing Bobbi, but they must've talked sometime. She calls herself Georgia West. Apparently she's local talent. There's only one problem . . . "

Restlessly, he rose and started for a walnut cabinet whose glass doors revealed two shelves lined with cognac. I got up to stretch my legs. Halfway across the room, Graves stopped, spun on his heels like a Little Theatre villain and in a voice dripping with drama said, "The day after the police talked to her, the hooker disappeared. Apparently, nobody's seen her since. So you're going to have to find her. She's my ace in the hole."

I didn't have time to applaud his performance.

A shrill shout erupted from the outer office—his secretary was no longer laid-back—and there were sounds of scuffling. The door of his office imploded.

"Graves, I'm going to destroy you! You're a murderer!" A skinny fellow in his thirties had shoved the secretary ahead of him and now stood yelling in the doorway to Graves' office. He had a halo of tight black curls and his eyes were wide-open behind rimless glasses. His right hand was waggling a gun up and down, wildly, as if it were a magic wand that would make Graves disappear. Maybe it would.

"Gold, what the hell! That's my gun. Put that down! You're drunk!" Graves was frozen beside the liquor cabinet across the room.

"You're going to die for what you did!"

Scared as I was, I couldn't help noticing that it sounded like a line from those old gangster movies I play on my VCR at 3:54 A.M. when I can't get back to sleep.

"What did I do?" Graves' voice vaulted from tenor to soprano.

"You killed my screenplay. My career. You . . . all of you"— he whipped the gun around in an arc that included the secretary and me (why me?)— "Cowan . . . Melts . . . *Bobbi* . . . even she wanted to destroy me. I'll *destroy you*." He was speaking in a slow slur now, quietly, which upset me more than his yelling. I decided that if I wanted this job, not to mention the rest of my life, I had better do something.

Gold, still in the doorway, still muttering a litany of threats and accusations, was focussed on Graves at the other end of the room. Carefully, carefully, I placed my hands on top of the leather chair I was standing beside. I gave it a sharp shove across the short-piled rug. The chair sped along on its casters towards Gold.

And stopped.

A foot away from him.

Oh hell.

Gold, distracted by the creak of the chair, turned. Looked at me blindly. Then rushed in my direction, brandishing the gun. He didn't see the chair. It caught him at the thighs and he fell on it in a bellyflop. The force of impact knocked the wind out of him. The revolver flew on towards me.

I picked it up from the rug. Gold rolled off the chair and on to the floor, where he began sobbing between gasps, looking about as threatening as a goldfish on grass. "That's mine," a flushed Graves told me, reaching out for the gun.

It was a Smith & Wesson, a stubby Model 36 Chief's Special. I broke it open and checked all five chambers. Not a single .38 Special cartridge inside. "Your gun wasn't loaded."

"No," he said, almost to himself. "No, it isn't."

3

Win One,
Lose One

❖❖

ithin minutes West Vancouver uniforms ar-
rived to pick up a quieter but still hysterical Burt Gold. Hearing
the bare bones of our stories, they decided he should go to
Riverview for psychiatric observation. As ambulance atten-
dants bundled him in a straitjacket, two middle-aged plainclothes began ninety minutes of extracting statements from
Adam Graves, his secretary and a security-company employee
who just happened to be on the scene. Apparently, from what
I could overhear from the outer office, they took special pains
to ask what an American movie producer was doing with an un-
registered Smith & Wesson. Graves said that after Bobbi's
murder, he'd got the revolver from one of the crew for self-
protection and Gold must have stolen it from his desk. When
the police left, with the gun and with Detective Frank Collins
warning me to keep my nether region clean, a shaky Graves
pulled out another bottle of Remy and poured two snifters.
This time I didn't refuse.

"So," he said after chugalugging the cognac, "Burt Gold. Who would have thought Gold was a killer."

"Is he?" If he was, he'd also murdered my chance to play detective.

"Looks like it, kid. He's been acting crazy for weeks."

"Well," I said, rising, "it's been . . . *fascinating* meeting you."

"Sit down. Just because I say he's a killer, there's no guarantee the damn cops will. I still want you to find Georgia West. Until they charge Gold, she's my only alibi. My insurance policy."

"I'll find her."

"Wonderful. Do it."

The Public Safety Building is conveniently located a short lurch down the block from its clients, the junkies and winos and strumpets voluntary who haunt Hastings Street. The Inspector in Major Crimes, which includes Homicide, is Phil Rusk. "Remove yourself from this office," he said by way of greeting.

He's the only cop I've ever met who collects antique west-coast Indian baskets. They're spotted around his office, gorgeous artifacts of grass and roots and rushes. With his pinched but intelligent face and his three-piece Ralph Lauren herringbones, Rusk looks like a corporation lawyer. An honest one. He smells of Aramis. Except when he smokes his cigars—which are purposely cheap and pungent, he once said, to insulate him from the stink of some of the places and people he encountered in his job. And here he was, pulling a cigar from his drawer.

"Inspector, I had nothing to do with that story."

"Your ladyfriend did, however. Leave, before I forget myself." I knew he was bluffing. I hoped I knew. As much as Rusk disliked me and my kind, as he would say, he loathed the narks who had embarrassed the force by cavorting like randy goats on the downtown rooftop.

"Inspector Rusk," I said, "I'm here in my official capacity as a properly licensed private investigator. I'm acting on behalf of a client who has hired me to help in the investigation of the murder of Bobbi Flynn. I'm asking you, as a member of the Vancouver city force, to extend any assistance you can." Somehow the tone of the monologue had sounded a hell of a lot more impressive when I'd memorized a version of it during my first week with TransWorld.

Rusk didn't snort in reply, of course. He wouldn't stoop to snorting or snarling. He sneered. "You will receive from me as much information about the Flynn case as you provided us about your ladyfriend's despicable intentions. In any event, what are you doing involving yourself in a murder? Doesn't TransWorld usually restrict itself to helping insurance companies avoid paying their customers? Don't you think your own time would be better spent guarding a construction site?"

"Didn't Carlyle say it's much easier to be critical than to be correct?" I was just baiting Rusk. I knew that he reads—real books—and prides himself on being an amateur historian.

He didn't disappoint me. "In fact, no: Disraeli said that." Whoops. "He also said if you're not very clever, you should be conciliatory."

"I'm trying, Inspector. All I want to know is whether you have any idea where I can find the prostitute who corroborated Adam Graves' alibi."

"Who's your client?"

"Graves."

"What does he want with . . . the prostitute?"

"He thinks she may have some leads for me."

"When we interviewed the subject for six and a half hours, no leads were forthcoming." Rusk seemed to be choosing his words carefully. "Moreover, we don't need this person anymore. And your client certainly doesn't need you."

"Why not?"

"We're about to lay a charge of murder in the Flynn case."

"Against whom?"

"Against Burt Gold."

From a pay phone down the street, I called the office. Surprisingly, I got right through to Jimmy Wright. But as I began to relate the morning's events, he interrupted: "What happened to the pictures on the stockbroker yesterday? You been working that job for a week." When I told him about the cops and the camera, he began to rage. "Goddam it, Rudnicki, you're off the job. Permanently. I've had it with you calling up and telling me you have to take your sick kid to the doctor. Or booking off early to go to some bloody school concert. And your relationship with the cops is crippling our investigations. Now you tell me you lost all the pictures of the guy changing his flat tire. We were already on probation with the insurance company. But the last bloody straw was breaking that camera of mine. That's it. I'll tell Graves we're replacing you, as of now."

Swell. I couldn't believe my day. I'm terrorized by a crazy carrying an empty gun. The cops announce that my first case is already solved, thank you very much. And I lose my steady job.

Yet when I called Graves to tell him I was unemployed, he only grunted and said: "Never mind being on the TransWorld payroll. I'll hire you freelance. I liked your style this morning. How much you going to charge me?"

The only figure that flashed through my mind was the full corporate fee Jimmy Wright charged me out at. "Three hundred and fifty a day—plus expenses," I said. Working it out later, I figured I could make $350 x 365 = $127,750 a year. Sure, or I could die of malnutrition.

"All right," Graves said. "So get moving on it."

"There's only one problem. The police have charged Gold with murder."

No response. Then: "Hell, that's no surprise. But anything can happen. I hired you to find the hooker. She's still my alibi. And she could have the answers to a lot of questions. Find her."

But first, to satisfy my curiosity, I would find out more about Adam Graves. I stopped by the Public Library downtown to see my friend Ann in Business Periodicals. We'd survived as friends since high school, despite my teenaged crush on her sable hair and ivory skin. I always sought her out whenever I needed help in the rare situation at TransWorld that required library research. A great gossip, like any good librarian, she demanded details of each case in return for her facts. Hearing my latest request, Ann smiled and said, "Give."

I gave enough dirt to satisfy her prurient nature.

Before scenting any fresh blood on the trail, she began by checking back ten years for periodical references on Graves. Together we went through the next five years, index after index of business and general publications, before we started picking up mentions of his name in the odd newspaper article. The first stories dealt with real-estate development in the New Jersey area. He was a bit player then, partner in a small shopping mall here, a four-storey office building there. These pieces in the dailies offered no background on Graves. He was a virtual nonentity until, after taking a stake in a major office tower in New York, he juggled a dazzling deal—buying his partners out and then flipping the property for nearly twice what they'd all paid for it. He'd used the profits as seed money to invest in a pharmaceutical company I'd never heard of before.

But the serious business press only deigned to anoint him with their attention when he began investing in off-Broadway plays. At the same time he was expanding westward, buying up buildings in St. Louis and Denver, and then moving on to Los

Angeles. It was there, in the Land of Deals on Wheels, that he became a minor presence in the media. In a year-old *Business Week*, Ann found an intriguing story on him:

Give Adam Graves credit for guts. As Hollywood's major studios were pulling in their horns in the wake of a disastrous Christmas season, the aggressive New York developer announced his impressive $19.5 million debut as an independent movie producer with a film featuring the hottest young starlet on the scene. "The Establishment guys are a little too gun-shy," says Graves, whose signing of former TV soap star Bobbi Flynn for a thriller called *The Empty Gun* is considered a coup in Los Angeles.

What's surprising old Hollywood hands is that Adam Graves has never made a movie before, yet has attracted such promising box-office material as Flynn and veteran actor Peter Cowan along with esteemed British director Robert Melts. For their part, members of the development community on the eastern seaboard expressed no surprise, knowing Graves' penchant for dealing well-heeled private investors in on his real-estate transactions, which invariably leave him holding the best cards.

For a budding Hollywood tycoon, Adam Brendan Graves seems to have a checkered past. He'll talk about his sometime backing of New York theatre and his success in syndicating property in the East. But aside from noting that he hails from the Southwest Side of Chicago, and studied business at Northwestern, he prefers to speak in the present and future tenses. In other areas, Graves is playing his new role in classic fashion. A self-confirmed bachelor, he's known for his short-term dalliances with some of the West Coast's more flamboyant beauties and for the elaborate parties at his Beverly Hills mansion.

Film insiders speculate that Graves may have called on some of his former property-development partners to invest in . . .

The story went on about how Graves was shooting on location in Vancouver to take advantage of the Canadian dollar. After

28

scanning a few other articles, which had no history of my new
client, I was ready to retire for the day. It was five o'clock and,
having faced a gun and the axe, I felt like one of Hannibal's
foot soldiers hiking the Alps. I was too wiped to swap the
measured security of my cedar-shake house in Kitsilano for a
Bryan Adams concert at the stadium downtown. Knowing it
was my father's bingo night, I called Nadia at the *Sun* and tried
to persuade her that attending a rock show with two barely
pubescent girls would give her an offbeat column. She went
only because she liked Esther and Larissa.

Later that night, I awaited their return in a serene house,
lolling in my long old claw-foot bathtub, sipping on a steamy
glass of Black Velvet, and smoking a guilty Craven "A" while
listening to k.d. warble "Down To My Last Cigarette." Shevchenko sat curled in the doorway, glowering at me. The girls'
ugly old ginger cat. I loathe cats—I hate any creature that can
be more independent than me. So when the kids begged me
to have one, I insisted on naming it. I christened him for
Ukraine's national poet because they had the same brooding
eyes and big whiskers. The cat has never forgiven me. My
daughters, of course, call him Shevvy.

It was nearly midnight when the door chime bonged. I
wrapped myself in a ratty robe to follow Shevchenko downstairs and greet Nadia and the girls.

"It was *ex*-cellent, Daddy," said Esther.

"It was bogus, Father," said Larissa.

I looked at Nadia. Her dark Ukrainian eyes lifted in suppli-
cation.

"Okay, kids, up to bed. It's late. Stay for a drink, Nadia."

"One."

At this hour of the night, it was always one. Long ago when
we were reporters on the student paper at Simon Fraser
University, we had a brief but sensational relationship. Nadia
Kulish had dunked me in a stew of causes: Greenpeace, SDS,
nuclear disarmament. She had a stronger stomach for it than

I did and in our last year we were no longer supping at the same table. Since then we'd had an Understanding. We were friends, even through my much-too-brief marriage to Sarah. And Nadia was there afterwards, after Sarah's death, through all those weeks and months as I passed from shock through despair to rage against the hit-and-run driver the police had never found. Nadge was the only one who could finally convince me to stop following up the slightest clue, to stop chasing after the person who'd killed my wife—to stop, and to start my life again, if only for Esther and Larissa. As my life tore at the seams, Nadia was always around to stitch it up.

But, with a few exceptions, her demonstrations of support always stopped at the bedroom door. Which pained me, when I was whole enough to think about it, because along with admiring her sexy mind, I lusted after her clever body. It was tall, three inches taller than mine. And dusky, more classically Slavic in skin coloring. And full, free of any sharp edges.

And off-limits.

"Okay, how was it for you?" I asked her.

"*Interesting*. I just might get a column out of tonight. But not about kids at a rock concert . . . Did you know your daughter Larissa is growing up very fast?"

I nodded. Did I. Not only physically, with blossoming florets of breasts and other, more subtle feminizing of her figure. But also in the way she was acting, and over-reacting to everyone, especially me. No more casual hugs. Lots more sudden detonations.

"She's almost a young woman, you know," Nadia said. "Her hormones are kicking in. And don't forget that 'estrogen' comes from Greek words that mean 'to produce mad desire.' She probably doesn't know what's happening to her. Has she talked to you about it?"

"Nadge, she only talks to me when she wants something or wants to complain about something at school."

"You've got to talk to her, Dan, or give her the opportunity

◆◆

to open up to you. She was hinting at all sorts of things with me tonight, boys and sex, things that I couldn't discuss in much detail because of Esther. Maybe sometime when we're alone."

"Lord, I'd appreciate it," I said, touching her cheek. "I'm just managing to tread water as their cook, clothier and zookeeper."

"Now tell me, in detail this time, why you couldn't take them to the concert," she said, reclining on the cinder-scorched Scandinavian rug in front of the livingroom fireplace.

I told her, in between putting some clothes on, building a fire, kissing the kids goodnight, going upstairs again to negotiate the nightly truce between them, shooing Shevchenko out of the room, and then pouring a rye for Nadia and slicing up garlic sausage to serve with a plate of my Dad's pickled beets.

When I finished the story, she asked softly, "When will you get a real job? As a reporter? Or a history teacher? Or a white slaver?"

Good questions. I couldn't give her an answer, but they were terrific questions. Anyway, she knew: my poli sci degree was intended to support a career in teaching, but when my interest in writing got me a spot on the university paper, I was hooked. All that hype about Woodward and Bernstein inspired me— me and my whole generation—to be an investigative journalist. My summers were spent trying to hone those investigative skills with a security job at TransWorld. Meanwhile, after the split with Nadia, I fell in love with a woman who shared my obsession with old movies and New Journalism, along with several of my courses at Simon Fraser. Sarah, the dark-haired lady with wealthy roots and a rich social conscience. We married a week after graduating.

Our honeymoon, on my meagre savings and her family's largesse, lasted nearly a year as we camped and hostelled across Europe, inhaling culture and falling further in love. It ended after we came home, with Sarah pregnant, when I couldn't get a job on any local paper I considered worthy of my talents.

31

Instead I wrote muckraking freelance pieces for the *Georgia Straight* and earned my full-time living as a private investigator with TransWorld. Meanwhile, we had a second daughter. Good as I was at security work, and good as the money became, the job was supposed to be a stopgap until a respectable reporting position surfaced. But after Sarah's death, I believed my work at TransWorld would put me in a better position to pursue the driver who'd killed her. Besides, the job offered the flexibility of hours that let me lavish time and attention on our young children. So why, Rudnicki, are you still using that as an excuse now—when the trail of Sarah's killer is stone-cold dead and the girls need you a whole lot less?

"Nadge, let's talk about something cheerful. Like salmonella."

"You're such a *smarkotch*." She always insulted me in Ukrainian. "But you're a nice man and it's your life, tawdry as it is. Except, my friend, this case you're on sounds a *teensy weensy* bit more dangerous than what you've been doing. And I've got another distasteful question for you: How are you going to find that missing prostitute for Graves?"

"I haven't got a clue. Maybe I can advertise in the Business Personals."

"*Teh doornay.* You dummy. Why don't you see Simone?" The prostitute I'd saved that night on the roof with the police.

"You give me the blind staggers. Brilliant." I bent over to give her a thank-you kiss. The fire was reddening her plump lips and they tasted of—garlic. "Stay here tonight," I said. A clear breach of our Understanding.

She rolled away from me and sat up, brushing a long lock of chocolate hair from her face. "No, Dan, I'm headin' home. As my old Ukrainian mother always says, somebody else's hearth can never be quite as warm as your own."

❖❖

4

Simone
Says

❖❖

If I twitted Simone about the last traces of her Quebecois accent, it was partly guilt, partly grudge. Like generations of Western Canadians, I had a *soupçon* of high-school French. Enough to decipher the prose on the back of a Corn Flakes box, but not enough to follow a soap on the local French-language TV station. I was with Anthony Burgess. He said spoken French sounded to him a lot like Eskimo, with words all stuck together like frozen shrimp heads.

So I winced when I phoned Simone and got her recorded voice with its purposely purple accent. I knew Simone well enough to realize she'd be sleeping in after a hard night at the orifice. Even though I postponed my call until ten, her phone was still on the answering machine. "It is Simone." The tones were gravelly, like the purring of a French-Canadian cat. "Now I'm occupied but later I will be 'appy to speak wit' you. Leave your first name and number please when you 'ear the beep."

◆◆

I decided to see 'er in person. She lived downtown in the West End. Seeing the faces of the singles who inhabit that forest of anonymous towers, I tend to agree with the graffiti I once spotted on the Burrard Street bridge: *Entering the Worst End.* Simone's mud-grey apartment building is a remnant of the old city, a low brick-and-timber Tudor across the street from English Bay Beach. Clambering out of the Mini, I was nearly steamrollered by a bearded jogger, islanded from the bother of real life by the earphones of his Walkman. I had to step around a popcorn man wheeling his stand into place on the sidewalk. On the lawn that slopes down to the sand and water, a silvered old lady was trying to shoo away the gulls hustling her bread crumbs from a honking gaggle of Canada geese.

One minute's work on the downstairs buzzer awoke Simone. "Oo is there?" the intercom wanted to know.

"Dan."

"Rudnicki?"

"Uh-huh."

"Come up."

Greeting me in her electric-red peignoir, she looked weary but wonderful. Her small body was plumping out and softening as it neared its forties, yet she still seemed unattainable, like your best friend's older sister. The difference was that Simone Pelletier could be attained, by select customers, for $400 a night. Fifty bucks more than I was charging Graves. And you could put it on your Visa.

"'Ow are Esther and Larissa?"

"Diff-ee-cult. But shar-ming."

"Oh, don't make fun of my phoney accent, Dan. My clientele loves it." She hadn't lived in Quebec since she was twelve.

Simone sat on a fat sofa adorned with doilies she'd crocheted herself. Her legs were folded under her, the seductive peignoir primly closed, as tempting as an unwrapped box of chocolates. When the girls were little, we'd lived in the apart-

34

ment across the hall. She'd been inviting them over for homemade cookies for three weeks before I realized that she wasn't supporting herself on a Canada Council grant. And by then Esther and Larissa had decided she was a neat lady.

"How's business?" I asked.

"The economy's good. Tourism is strong, there's a lot of offshore investment in town, and we're the first to feel it. Me, I'm up about two thou a month. Even my computer stock's been trading high. It better be: the taxman is after me. They're still not letting me declare all my expenses. Like the fancy clothes I have to buy the odd time my clients actually want to see me all dressed up and show me off for the evening. My lawyer's thinking of taking my case all the way to the Supreme Court." She smiled at how long her stream of consciousness had been flowing. "So how's the security business? Do you want some breakfast?"

"No, but I'll watch." I followed her to the Colonial-style kitchen, watching. She slinked as she walked. Unconsciously: it was in her genes. "Business has picked up, actually," I said. "I left TransWorld and I'm on my own." I explained the events of the past eventful day.

"Dan," she said, "when are you going to get a decent job?"

"Not you too, Simone. Look, I need your help. Graves wants me to find a hooker that Bobbi used."

"Bobbi Flynn was gay? How disgusting."

"You should have listened to your folks and become a Sister of the Sacred Heart. Bobbi was bi. Anyway, the lady's name is Georgia West."

"Oh, Georgie. George. He's no lady. He's got one more operation to go before he becomes Georgia. But he looks good already. Good enough to eat, but don't bother trying yet. Well, I heard he'd been off the street for a few days. I didn't know why."

"The guy's a transsexual? Rusk didn't tell me that. As a matter of fact, neither did Adam Graves."

"Oh, yes." She buzzed some frozen grapefruit juice and water in her blender, poured the froth in a glass and drank it daintily as she told me why George's beauty wasn't even skin-deep.

"He looks like Margot Kidder. You know: long dark hair, good facial bones. I bet he looks *merveilleux* in black-net stockings. He's had all the hormones—*mon Dieu*, I wish I had as much estrogen as they've been pumping him full of. He's developing nice little boobs too, I hear. But I can't stand the thought of what he had done between his legs."

We moved back into the livingroom. Simone sat stiffly on the sofa, her hands protectively covering her crotch. "They cut it off. The whole thing: balls and cue. One of my girlfriends saw what's left. She says it looks a lot like ours and he pees like us, but he can't make it with a man."

"No room at the in?"

She groaned. My sense of humour goes all to hell when I'm absorbing uncomfortable facts. "So now George wants to go all the way and get a phony vagina."

Her phone rang. "'allo? Oo is it? Mm, hi there Gerry . . . Down how many points? . . . *Sell* . . . No, I'm booked tonight. How about Thursday?" Hanging up, she muttered, "My broker."

"What I need from you, Simone, is the likely whereabouts of George. Where does he/she hang out?"

He had a pimp, it turned out, a large tough boyfriend who oversaw the hustling George did to finance the surgery that wasn't covered by government medicare. Donny Breen could usually be found at a club for transsexuals, transvestites and others in transition. Meg's, on Seymour Street, one of the choicer slices of Vancouver's tenderloin. Simone sent me home with a virtuous kiss on the cheek and two hand-embroidered kerchiefs for Esther and Larissa.

❖❖

My old man caught me faking an early dinner for the girls. Frozen, store-bought perogies. "*Oy, Bohz-yeh!*" he said, taking the Ukrainian Lord's name in vain. "Why don't you ask, Dan? I made some sauerkraut ones, some potato-and-cheese, on Sunday. Don't waste your money on that stuff."

I inherited my height. Taras Rudnicki always reminded me of a stunted jockey, bent and bow-legged, and as hard and brittle on the outside as he was soft and malleable inside. He'd been retired from the railroad for seven years, since his Julia died, and it was no coincidence that he now lived a scant two blocks from the kids and me. I'd decided to tell him as little as possible about my new job: he worried like a *Baba*.

"So you're out again tonight? Who's looking after the girls?" he chided, nodding at his granddaughters, now in the kitchen with us, setting the table after being told to three times.

"Oh, Grampa," Larissa groaned, "I don't need anyone to look after me anymore."

"Neither do I," said Esther, not to be outdone.

He threw up his hands. "They're still little girls, Danylo. How can you just walk out and leave them?"

"Dad, Larissa goes out and baby-sits for other people. She's thirteen, going on thirty. She's a big girl now. And so is S.T.," I added hastily, using the family nickname for Esther.

"I'm not doing anything tonight," he said. The girls exchanged looks, their emotions probably caught between enjoying their grandfather's company and wanting to establish their feminist credentials. "I'll stay and watch TV. When will you get a colour set? It's a sin to watch Dolly Parton in black and white." We shared a fondness for country and western, although I leaned more to the esoteric, like the country-punk of k.d.

I could see Larissa sizing up the situation, the prospect of an unforeseen evening of freedom. "Then I'm going over to Kerry's after dinner, Dad," she said.

"Not at that hour, you're not."

Her hazel eyes flashed, which was always a warning. "You just said I was a *big* girl."

I was treading into a quagmire. Lately Larissa was about as predictable as Eastern Europe. "A big, growing girl who needs her beauty sleep on a school night. And who hasn't even practised her piano yet."

"Shit!" She began to flounce from the kitchen, leaving her grandfather aghast. "My *mother* wouldn't make me a prisoner in my own house."

She knew how to hurt. "One, Young Lady: you will not use that language in my presence. Two: I'm sorry your mother isn't here to make the rules. And three: even if she were, they'd be the same rules. Trust me, she'd be tougher than I am." Oh, Sarah, why couldn't you be here?

Larissa, her dudgeon in high gear, banged up the stairs and slammed her bedroom door hard enough to make the whole house shudder. She later graced us with her presence for dinner only after her grandparent went up to work out a cease-fire agreement. The terms did not include any further communications with me for the duration of the evening.

After dinner, as Larissa silently, seethingly, loaded the dishwasher, the ever-hopeful Esther asked for my help with her math homework. Ten minutes later I was asking for my father's help. "That's all right, Daddy," Esther said, patting my hand to soothe me. I left them poring over percentages and, with a freshet of rain pouring over the city, drove down Granville, across the bridge and into the downtown battleground of Seymour.

5

Hustling

The last time I'd walked the street, a sniper with a rifle poking out the back of a Granville hotel had pretended that he was a duck hunter. And I was a mallard until the cops convinced him I was out of season. Body shops and car dealerships share Seymour with the Penthouse strip club and the gently rocking RVs, parked at meters, where the more creative prostitutes take their clients. On the side streets, the sad little boys were out tonight, as every night. The fifteen-year-old male hookers wiggled their bums at their customers from the suburbs of Surrey and Coquitlam. Sad middle-aged men cruised by in their Malibus like floats in a sleazy parade.

I found a parking spot on an isolated lot where muggers liked to waylay drunken Yugoslav and Filipino sailors on shore leave from their ships. The rain had stopped but a hawk-nosed woman, shrouded in black, walked by with her torn umbrella splayed open. She was murmuring curses at the wicked fornicators who were overpopulating the world. In spring, the city's street crazies blossom as brilliantly as its Japanese flowering cherry trees.

Meg's had a discreet blue-neon sign announcing itself to the world, or to that exclusive part of it that an alternative club considered its clientele. A beach ball of a bouncer inside the door looked like a man at first glance. On the second I noticed that the chubby face under the greasy ducktail had distantly feminine features and not a whisper of a whisker. "Do we know you?" she wanted to know.

"You don't, but I'm a friend of Donny's. Donny Breen."

"He's not here."

"Well, he's late then. He's always late." As if I knew all about my old buddy Breen.

"Okay. Pay your five dollars. I'll check with Donny when he shows up."

A poster of a pouting Brando as The Wild One dominated the back wall of the low-lit room. Above the long burnished mahogany bar another flashing blue-neon sign winked *Make Me An Offer I Can't Refuse.* Most of the crowd looked respectably middle-class. But to reach the lone empty table in the back of the club, I had to survive a giggling gauntlet of punks in stovepipe pants, their hair a black forest of spikes. They cased me openly as I wriggled my way through the crowd. I felt as out of context as a red-coated Mountie at a Mafia funeral. With my high acne-scarred cheeks and Tartar's slant to my blue eyes, I wasn't even cute.

At the next table, well within touching distance, two taut-skinned young men in classic silk shirts over versatile white Polo pants were discussing Epstein-Barr's syndrome.

"You free?" He was a wide guy in a black-leather jacket, a decade younger than me. Or, judging by the junkheap of his face, maybe a century older. "Waiting for somebody?"

"Donny Breen."

"Breen? That big bastard? You like it rough? I'll give you rough, man." He sat down beside me, haunch to haunch.

"Actually," I said, moving away discreetly, "I'm trying to track down one of Breen's girls."

"You straight?" He stared at me as if I were a one-legged leper.

"My two daughters think I am. Look, I'm not cruising, I'm trying to find someone. George—*Georgia* West. And I'm not a john looking for some transsexual transaction. And I'm not a pimp, not a jilted lover, not a pusher and not a nark. I'm a private detective—"

"A private dick? In this place, they're all public." He snickered. "So why do you want Georgia?"

"Do you know her?"

"Yeah, I know *him*. He's Breen's favourite because he looks so good. He even got a *Province* photographer to take his picture looking like a broad and put it in 'Today's Smile.' Fooled all those straight jerks. Breen likes him because he works real hard to raise the bread for his operations. But he hasn't been around for days. I heard he's in trouble with the cops."

"Know why?"

"Nah. Except one night in here I heard Georgia talking to Breen about messing around with Bobbi Flynn—that movie star that got sliced up."

"What else did you hear? It's important."

"Yeah? How important?"

I'd seen the same bad movie. I pulled out my wallet and extracted a twenty-dollar bill.

Snatching at it with the speed of an undernourished barracuda, he said, "All I can remember is that Georgia was bitching it was tough trying to make it with another transsexual."

"You mean bisexual."

"Bisexual, transsexual—whatever."

Bored, he began looking around the room, his dark eyes flicking back and forth like a metronome on allegro. My new friend had the attention span of a backward two-year-old. I had to hurry: "When did you overhear this?"

"The last time I saw Georgia. Two weeks ago. A couple of nights before they found Flynn. And that was the last time I saw Donny Breen—which is good news."

"Why?"

"Breen's an animal. He doesn't care how he hurts you. He grabs whatever's around and uses it as a weapon. He once put a guy's hand in a blender and turned it on to Liquefy. You better have a good reason for wanting Georgia or Breen'll make blood soup out of your face."

"So," I enquired delicately, "is there any way of finding Georgia West without going through Donny Breen?"

"I doubt it. Unless you spot Georgia's grundgy green Buick on the street. It's got one of those message license plates."

"What does it say?"

"HUSTLE."

What the heck. That was enough of a lead to go on. I could see Donny Breen another night when I didn't mind becoming the stock for his blender soup. Standing up, I asked, "What's your name?"

"Timmy."

Before I could say goodbye to Timmy, he was at the next table trying to intrude on the classic silk shirts. The tramp.

❖❖

On the way home that night I made a couple of detours. The first was to see the dispatcher at Kits Cabs. I'd driven on weekends for old Mickey several summers ago when I was trying to swell the size of the down payment for the house—most of it from Sarah's life insurance, a poignant legacy.

"Dan, my man," Mickey said, "you coming back to push hack?"

"Sure. I really miss sitting at the airport doing crossword puzzles for five hours a night. Cleaning up the vomit in the back seat. Getting knifed in the nose. Actually, Mick, I need your help." I took out another twenty—leaving myself with ten—and gave it to Mickey. I asked him to get on his radio with a description of Georgia West's green Buick with the HUSTLE plate. And to tell his sixty-seven drivers there was fifty bucks for anyone who phoned me immediately at home or at the film studio with the exact location of the car.

I also stopped in at an eclectic video store, my second home, to pick up Bobbi Flynn's obscure first movie. My father began watching it with me but soon left, shaking his head and lamenting aloud his son's taste for sleaze and violence. *Scorcher* was a no-name action picture with a frail plot hanging on the escapades of a couple of male-buddy firemen during one long hot summer in San Francisco. Bobbi was the girl caught between them. The lone critical excerpt on the video jacket quoted Roger Ebert: "Bobbi Flynn scorches the screen . . . . " She did sizzle. All that summer heat encouraged her to loll around in little more than suntan oil and a string bikini, exposing perhaps the most perfect breasts since Marilyn's. Yet hers wasn't a sunny, open beauty. There was a dark, feral quality to it, dangerous, daring you to touch—and risk burning yourself on her red, hot flesh.

❖❖

6

Body
Check

❖❖

The girls woke me with a cup of coffee, a bribe
to con me into letting them sleep over at Sarah's parents' place
on the weekend. Unasked, Larissa even threw in a good-
morning kiss, as if last night had just been a bad dream. It all
worked.

I dropped them off at school, en route to Cypress Studios.
The grassy shoulders of the road through Stanley Park wore
yellow epaulets of spring daffodils. There was a scent of pine
and Douglas fir in the silky morning air. And I was going to see
a man about a murder.

Adam Graves greeted me as if I'd committed the murder.
"Have you found Georgia West yet?"

"Not yet. I usually take two days to locate transsexuals. I
never know whether to look for them in the ladies' or the
men's room."

That stopped him. He merely looked at me. Finally he

spoke. "Who said anything about transsexuals?"

"You didn't. And the police didn't. But a prostitute and a guy in a bar did. Apparently George West decided to surrender his gender and become a she-male. Didn't you know?"

He paused. "How would I know?"

Who answers rhetorical questions? Instead, I told him I had several other operatives looking for Georgia and, meanwhile, maybe I should be making my investigative presence felt to reduce the level of paranoia at the studio.

"I'm paying you to find West—"

His intercom interrupted. "Barney O'Malley is here," his secretary said.

"All right."

A man in his late fifties waddled in like a force-fed goose. But from a look at his booze-ravaged complexion, I guessed that Barney O'Malley's liver would make a lousy *foie gras*.

"Barney's our senior publicist on the picture," Graves said. He must have been the one who fed the *Province* the angle about Burt Gold's arrest: CRAZED WRITER PULLS EMPTY GUN ON 'EMPTY GUN' PRODUCER. "This is the detective I told you about—Rinicky."

"Dan Rudnicki," I corrected, shaking O'Malley's spongy hand.

"Danny boy, you're just the fella I need," the publicist said. He lowered his bulk into a chair, the fat rippling out of his blue-ticking-striped shirt. His yellow bowtie bounced up and down his hamhock of a neck with every word he spoke. "Everybody is still antsy on the set. A lot of people had a lot of time for Burt Gold. You and I may think different, Adam, but nobody else really wants to believe he could murder anything but a screen-play. Why don't we have Danny here hang around today? Maybe speak to a few people. Let them think we're still concerned. Cowan is threatening to walk out, he's so upset. We can't afford to lose another day. Not when we're still looking for four and a half mil."

"Just what I was suggesting," Graves lied. "Listen, kid, they're shooting outdoors today. Cowan has only a few lines in the scene so go talk it up with him and make him feel better. Tell him what happened with Gold, let him know they got the right guy."

Barney O'Malley stank of sour Scotch. "So you're a private detective, Danny. Good money?" he said as we walked outside. "I bet you don't get many cases up here like this one. I got a friend, used to be on the L.A. force, who's private now. Works for the studios, finds lady stars who don't show up on the lot for two weeks. Usually finds them shacked up with some stud, going through a case of coke. You wearing your gun?"

"I don't own one," I squeezed in.

"Christ, that's Canada for you. I bet you don't even cross against a red light either. I don't know anybody in California who doesn't have a gun. My brother the priest packs one. I can't understand you people. Don't you have any sense of . . . of personal freedom?"

"Sure, we like the freedom of staying alive."

"Hey, owning a gun is one of your basic rights. Like owning a car."

"And everybody who owns a car has to pass a test proving he knows how to use it. And he has to register the car and have a license number so the police know who's driving it. That's a lot more than you have to do in the States to own a gun."

"Okay, here's the set," he said, dismissing me and my lecture. "I'll tell Melts you're gonna be here today. Better stick around for the whole shoot."

The set was the flat of a pawnbroker's shop that I'd seen the other day. A crowd scene, a dozen men and women idling around the storefront while the camera and sound crews tuned their equipment. The bearded Robert Melts, built like a buddha but gesturing like a southern preacher, was leaning into Peter Cowan, costumed in an olive trenchcoat.

"You've precisely *seven* lines in this scene, Peter, and you

47

have managed to mangle four of them in the past twelve takes."
The director's voice was a stage whisper that projected to
downtown Vancouver.

"If you could make up your bloody limey mind how you want
to shoot this scene, Melts, we would've finished an hour ago."

"Let us do it once again. Properly, this time," Melts said
quietly, retreating behind the camera. He almost backed into
me. "*Who* is this person?" he demanded.

"Bob, it's the private detective," Barney O'Malley said.
"Adam said it was okay. He wants a word with Peter when he's
free."

"Perhaps he'll have better luck getting Cowan to speak
without stumbling over his lines. In the meantime, have this
man remove his jacket and join the extras at the left of the
door. That area wants filling out. We'll take care of the union
paperwork afterwards. *You*"—he pointed at me—"are one of
the passersby who witness Mr. Cowan accosting a hoodlum on
the street. Let me see. You are of the lower classes, a greengrocer's clerk, on your way to luncheon, and you will appear
surprised yet fascinated by the little drama playing before
you."

My big break. Me, playing a fully fleshed grocery clerk in the
movies.

For the next half-hour I was surprised yet fascinated as
Cowan blew his lines three more times. I didn't realize "scumbag" had so many pronunciations.

As I was lounging in the sun between takes, filling out a
union card for temporary work, a man dressed exactly like
Cowan sidled up to me. His hair was styled to resemble the
star's, but his fiftyish face was leaner and crosshatched by lines
and scars. "You the private cop?"

When I nodded, he stuck out one rope-veined hand. "Leo
Garnett. Cowan's stunt double. I hear you helped take down
Burt Gold when he attacked Graves. Great stuff. But I still can't
figure Burt for a murderer."

"Thanks. It was nothing. And to tell the truth, Leo, I didn't have much time to get to know Burt. But from what I've heard, he was in bad shape."

"Yeah, he was as skittery as a bronc busting out of the chute. He wasn't eating, he couldn't sleep. Then he just seemed to get weird, thinking everyone was against him. The poor paranoid bastard even talked about people talking to him from the TV. And now they say he's a murderer. So what are you still doing on the case?"

"I'm here to somehow reassure Peter Cowan that everything's fine. Do you know him very well?"

He gave me a slow smile. "*Very* well. I've done the gags on three of his pictures." I had seen *Doublecross* on video so I asked if he'd done the stunt where Cowan knocked the revolver out of the villain's hand with a shoulder-high drop kick. Leo had. It turned out that after coming off a Saskatchewan farm he'd been a second-round draft choice in the AFL and punted a couple of years in Los Angeles before getting into stunt work with Hal Needham, the highest-paid stunt man in the business.

Settling in to talk, he perched his six-foot frame on a sawhorse, careful not to get his gabardine trenchcoat dirty. "I've done thirty-seven pictures now, but I'll tell you, nothing touches this one for trouble. You get a feeling on the first few days of a shoot. I knew this was going to be bad from the start."

"Oh?"

"Oh, yes. Everyone was as tight as a bull's ass. Bobbi Flynn couldn't stand Peter right from Day One. I think she resented the fact he was a big name and she wasn't. Typical of the kids coming in to the game nowadays. Everything has to be instant: just add water, stir, and you're a star."

"What did Cowan think of her?" I asked as lightly as I could.

Leo fixed me with his hooded little farmhand's eyes, slitted by years in the sun and wind. The pause was pregnant enough to deliver a baby rhino. Obviously deciding he could trust me, he said, "He liked her a whole lot less than she liked him."

49

"Did she know that?"

He let out a long, rusty chuckle. "Oh, did she ever. She caught him telling Bob Melts that the only acting she ever did was on her back. He thought she was as dumb as a sack of hammers."

Leo was about to go on when Melts' voice rang out: "Righto, that's a wrap." Peter Cowan began walking away without a word —he'd used them all up trying to say "scumbag." With a wave and a "See you later" to Leo, I grabbed my jacket and ran after him.

"Mr. Cowan. Dan Rudnicki. Can I talk to you?" I was gasping for breath as I ran. It was my allergies. Either that or the smoking or the fact that I was wearing eight extra pounds. Fortunately, Cowan stopped.

"I'm tired, Rudnicki. Tired and distraught and impatient. I hope this is important."

"It is."

"I'll give you a few minutes. We'll talk in my trailer."

It was a boxy Atco construction-camp trailer, aluminum-sided, making up for its lack of exterior stylishness with its fifty-foot length and homey lakeside-cabin interior. Lace curtains on the windows, twin sofas of real leather, and a microwave and dishwasher in the pine-lined kitchen. He left the door open, which suggested either that he wasn't about to tell me anything others couldn't overhear or that he didn't expect me to stay long.

Cowan, sweating, stripped off his trenchcoat. As he went to hang it up, his eyes flicked to something on a kitchen counter. He walked over and tried to cover it with a tea kettle, as if he were tidying up. All I could see was what looked like the cover of a magazine.

We settled uneasily into the sofas, across from one another, as taut as a couple of hockey players about to face off. It began innocently enough as I tried to break the ice by asking if he'd made many movies in Canada since leaving for the States. A few, he replied—but moving south had been the best decision he'd ever made. And wasn't it a mockery that some misguided Canadian quasi-intellectuals were worried about the cultural effects of the free-trade agreement between the two countries. When I suggested that free trade might dilute Canadian culture to a bland and watery brew, he pshawed. He'd spent a lot of time on the Continent, and the Common Market hadn't weakened the cultures of all those countries. When I said those countries were protected by different languages and centuries of their own traditions, he smirked and wondered what truly unique culture Canada had to protect. And when I said that maybe if actors like him would stay home and make movies that reflected the Canadian psyche, instead of running up here to knock off violent flicks about American cops and robbers, the tension between us became thick enough to stand on.

"Did you simply come here to badger me, Rudnicki?" he demanded in a portentous voice that smacked more of over-baked Hollywood ham than the rare Hamlet I'd seen him do at the Stratford Festival a dozen years ago.

Which gave me my opening. I apologized, and mentioned his Hamlet admiringly, and watched his actor's ego swell almost visibly. He was softened up enough for me to ask: "Did Burt Gold really do it?"

"Well, of course he did. The man was the only one with reason to. And he was almost the only likely candidate who wasn't at the dailies."

"Dailies?"

"The rushes. The unedited film from the day's shoot. I was at the dailies, along with Melts and almost everyone else, all during the time the police established that Bobbi was killed. Gold wasn't there. And he was suffering a severe nervous breakdown."

"Why?"

"I knew when I accepted this role that the script had holes in it large enough to herd an elephant through." (*Yeah,* I

51

thought, *or even your ego.*) "I knew I would be making changes throughout the shooting. What I didn't realize is how many would be necessary. Near the end, Gold was on the run, finding it impossible to meet my standards and angered at having to. Then, when Bobbi began making her own demands of his script, Burt Gold simply snapped."

"Sounds reasonable. But was he the only one who had a hate on for Bobbi?"

"Hate on or hard on?"

Hey, puns were my territory. "I gather you were not enamoured of her."

"And who, may I ask, implied that?" he enquired, dramatically.

"I inferred it," I replied, grammatically.

He rose and went to the full-sized fridge, fetching and pouring himself a Perrier. Oh, no thanks, Peter, none for me, I'm fine.

"Bobbi Flynn and I may have had the odd difference of opinion, but our relationship remained entirely professional throughout."

"I understand you hated her acting."

"Where are you acquiring your information?"

"Why are you answering me with questions?"

"Now hear this, my man," Cowan said, in the tone he probably perfected chewing out Melts. "Although Bobbi was a fledgling, I respected her native energy and appreciated how the camera captured her beauty. She was an asset to this picture, and if that fool Melts or anyone has told you I felt anything different, he's a goddamned liar."

"I haven't talked to Melts. Yet."

He threw back his Perrier, almost choking on it. "Well, when you do," he said, moving to the open door, willing me to leave, "ask him about Jennie."

Taking the hint, I stood up and followed him. No chance to see what he'd been trying to conceal in the kitchen. "Jennie who?"

"Jennie Barlow. Bobbi's personal manager. If you're collecting suspects, you might want to talk to her."

"Why?" I asked, stepping outside into the sun.

"Because," he said, as he closed the door on me, "Jennie wasn't at the dailies. Bobbi had fired her just a few days before the murder."

Oh.

❖❖

7

Out with
Flynn

❖❖

Stuff Graves and O'Malley and their wanting me to stand around asking questions to make people feel better. Leo Garnett told me where Jennie Barlow was staying, a condo above False Creek. One of those swell-looking but ticky-tacky clusters of fashionable townhouses that climb the south-slope hills above the saltwater inlet which slices through downtown. Hers was pastel-blue and indistinguishable from its neighbours, except for the brass-plated numbers of its address. But it sat only a few hundred yards from the water, where a small village of sailboats rocked at anchor, creating a view that allowed developers to tack on tens of thousands of dollars to the price of each False Creek condo.

I'd called to see if Jennie Barlow was in, told her I was investigating Bobbi's murder and wondered if she could answer a few basic questions. Sure, such as: Did she do it?

She had told me, in what sounded like New York nasal, that she was in no shape to answer any more questions. When I'd persisted, telling her I had some information she might be interested in (I wondered what that might be), she relented.

Her face fit her voice, but her body didn't. She had hair the color of pitch, cut short and curled in corkscrews, and features that were as sharp and clipped as her accent. Yet an intelligent and not unattractive forty-year-old face, with wide brown eyes that were out of character with the rest of the physiognomy. And the kind of body that always brought out the big brother in me, wanting to enfold it in my arms: compact, not more than five-two, softly rounded in black wool pants and fluffy black-and-white sweater. In this case, it was the incestuous big brother coming out in me. She reminded me, in size and personal style, of Sarah. As she greeted me at the door, I had to remind myself that she might be a murderess.

"Excuse the mess," she said, ushering me up the three steps to a livingroom, "but I'm getting ready to head back to New York." The centre of the room was choked with suitcases, clothing, and filing folders. Skirting the edges, she sat down and pointed me to an armchair that shouted Furniture Rental. It felt as comfortable as it looked. I winced as I sat. If only I'd taken care of my back, the way my mother had always warned me, God rest her nagging soul.

My mother would not have approved of the way I was gazing at Jennie Barlow. Damn, her eyes were so much like Sarah's, like chestnuts freshly shiny from their husks. Finally embarrassed at my silent stare, she almost harrumphed as she asked: "What exactly did you have to tell me, Mr. Rudnicki?"

She got more marks for pronouncing the name right. "We'll get to that. It's more what I had to ask you, Ms Barlow." I hoped she didn't miss the "Ms."

"I guess the first thing I'd like to know is what, in fact, are you investigating? If it's Bobbi's terrible death, haven't the police solved that?"

"They think they have. Do you?"

She thought before she spoke. Which endeared her to me even more. "I was an admirer of Burt's work, if not his personality," she began. "Oh, he was always temperamental, but he had the talent to justify it. Naturally, he got upset when everybody started dumping on his script—I tried getting Bobbi to back off, to not much avail. Still, Burt was handling his anger professionally enough. He seemed fine, he told me he was sleeping through the night. Then a few weeks ago, he seemed to crack. He couldn't remember things, he seemed depressed, he began accusing people of outrageous actions. He'd become a stranger. For all that, I'm just not sure I believe he killed Bobbi. But if the police believe it, what are you doing?"

"Wrapping up some loose ends for my client. Adam Graves."

"Oh, Adam." Her face turned unattractive as she spoke his name.

"You have some problem with Graves?"

"No more than most people. I hate to tell you this, but your client was a bastard to Bobbi. I was pushing her agent in L.A. to renegotiate our contract with him when poor Bobbi . . . died."

"Agent?"

"One of the dozens of faceless junior agents at William Morris, who took his ten per cent for crossing the Ts on the deals that I really found for her as her personal manager."

"And how much do you take?"

"Fifteen . . . Anyway, Adam was about as tractable as a concrete block. He wouldn't entertain paying her another nickel, even though her first picture had come out after he'd signed her for *The Empty Gun* and she'd gotten all those rave reviews. Unfortunately, Bobbi didn't believe I was pushing hard enough."

"Is that when she fired you?"

Jennie Barlow's chestnut eyes dropped fifty degrees in

warmth. "Yes," she said tersely. "Not many people know that. I suppose Adam told you."

"No, not Adam."

"So I gather that if he and you believe that Burt Gold didn't . . ." She paused to regroup: "If Burt isn't guilty, then, in your eyes, maybe I am?"

"No, I'm not suggesting that," I said, although of course I was. "But there have been questions raised, Jennie. May I call you Jennie? Questions such as: if you weren't at the dailies the night of Bobbi's death, where were you?"

As she pondered her reply, I watched those doe eyes for a flicker of anxiety. They continued to stare at me, unblinking. Either she was a better actress than Bobbi or she wasn't about to dissemble when she answered me. "I really have no alibi," she said eventually. "I was right here, deciding what to do with the rest of my life. If you must know, I was drinking too much Scotch and crying my eyes out."

Her large eyes looked as if they were about to brim again. I felt the big brother rising in me once more, but I worried that if I ever put my arms around her it wouldn't be the only thing that would rise. Lord, maybe I wouldn't be this frustrated if Nadia and I got it on as well as we got on.

"And no," Jennie was saying, "I didn't . . . *harm* Bobbi. Yes, we had a monumental argument. She raged at me, told me I didn't know how to handle Adam or her agent, but she knew how to change Adam's mind, she knew where he was most vulnerable, and she no longer needed me—she was firing me. But no, I did not harm her. In my own way, I quite loved the silly little bitch. After all, Mr. Rudnicki, I helped create her."

"*Dan* — please. Jennie, sorry I'm upsetting you even more with all these questions," I said gently in my best bedside manner. "I want to get to the bottom of this mess. I'm not so sure that Burt Gold isn't guilty, but if he isn't, I think you'd want to know just who is as much as I would. Maybe it would help if you told me something about Bobbi's background. *How did you help create her?*"

Jennie sighed, wrapped her arms tightly around her doll-like frame and seemed to shrink into herself. Her voice had lost some of its hard Manhattan edge when she said: "You seem like a decent enough guy, Dan. If you're really interested in Bobbi, and you're not just pimping for Adam Graves, I'll tell you what I can. But can we get out of this place for a while? I'm becoming claustrophobic looking at all my suitcases."

"Sure. Do you want to wander down to Granville Island and have a coffee?"

"Let's."

We stepped into the soft April afternoon and sauntered silently down the hill and across car-clogged Fourth Avenue to the sidewalk leading to the Island. We seemed to have an unspoken understanding: no speaking until we sat down together. The sun felt soothing on my back as we moved onto the boardwalk beneath the vaulting concrete piers of the Granville Street bridge. The Island is more of an isthmus, where the old factories and warehouses have surrendered to an armada of restaurants and theatres, artsy studios and crafty shops, and a sprawling public market. We wended our way through the covered market, through thickets of shoppers sizing up the whole salmon on ice, savouring the bouquet of fresh oregano, and picking over hillocks of spring-fresh yellow Gala apples. Jennie's mouth, which was a little moue in repose, flashed into full smiles at the sights and scents. We fetched cappuccinos and fat bran muffins and sat at an outdoor table overlooking False Creek and a pair of jugglers tossing around sharp knives and dull jokes.

"It's nice," Jennie said, leaning back into her chair, licking the froth from her coffee. "After everything that's happened the past ten days, I need this. God, it's been horrible. Poor Bobbi."

"Poor you, too. Whether Bobbi lived or died, you were out of a job."

"Oh, I'll survive, Dan. I've been in the management game too long to let the loss of one client destroy me. I'll go back to New York and pick up where I left off before Bobbi came into my life. In any case, I've got three other young actors in my stable, doing soaps."

"Isn't that where Bobbi started? In soap operas?"

Her eyes, framed by cobwebs of fine wrinkles that I could see in the sunlight, seemed to look inward, remembering. Maybe she was ready to unburden herself of the nightmare by telling Bobbi's story aloud in the bright glare of daytime. "She came out of Des Moines, Iowa. Roberta Flynn. She did some model-ling in her hometown and that filled her head with the idea of becoming an actress. She used to see road-show productions in Des Moines and got big eyes for the stage. So, all of eighteen, she came to New York, changed her name to Bobbi, went on the cattle-call circuit, and at some point picked my name out of the phone book. My secretary let her in to see me and I got Bobbi her first bit part in *All Our Tomorrows*. The soap audience adored her. She was so exquisite—I'll always remember, *Newsweek* said she was 'a pocket-sized, eighties version of Rita Hayworth.' The fact that she had no real training, no desire to learn her craft, didn't seem to matter. When the cameras came on, she . . . *scintillated*."

"Speaking of sin," I said, with the clumsiest of transitions, "she did have a certain reputation. I gather she was no saint."

"Christ." Jennie bit her little lower lip. "She can't escape it, even in death. There are no saints, Dan. Only fanatics with good press agents. Yes, it's true, she could have stepped right out of a Jackie Collins novel. She was very hungry for attention, for fame, and the trade-off for her lack of talent was one long casting couch. The classic story, dammit. And the wretched thing, Dan, is that she didn't really like men. She much preferred women as sexual partners. She came from a family where the mother was a wimp and the father was abusive—incestuously so, I always suspected, though Bobbi never admitted that. Anyway, he deserted them both when she was nine."

One of the jugglers dropped a knife. We both stopped talking to watch him recover, missing only a beat or two. When she refused my offer of a Craven "A", I lit up one for myself. "Does everyone famous have to spring from an infamous childhood?" I said, making conversation as Jennie washed her muffin down with coffee.

"In Bobbi's case," she said, "it seemed to give her the drive to escape the past . . . and a . . . a kind of amorality that allowed her to manipulate people to make sure she succeeded, fast. I felt some of that from the beginning, when she joined me—incredibly captivating and agreeable one moment, then hard and demanding the next. There wasn't much of a honeymoon between us before she started trying to run the show."

"And did she?"

"Fortunately, I had the contacts and she wasn't yet known, so she had to listen. But then she decided to make her own contacts—and *make* is the operative word. She was staying at my apartment for a couple of weeks when she was between places. I came home early one afternoon and found her on the livingroom floor with a producer of *All Our Tomorrows*. This was before she had a lead part."

"What were they doing?" I asked idly. Or so I thought.

"You *really* want to know, Dan? Is this a professional question or just plain voyeurism?"

"Actually, a little of both. It may give me some insight into the woman."

"It might, at that. The guy was on the floor, trussed like the pig he was, and Bobbi was straddled over him, squatting, administering what the skin mags euphemistically refer to as a golden shower. And he was loving it."

"Glad I asked."

"Yes, well, at least she had the decency to spread *The New York Times* over my carpet first. I turned on my heel and walked out, and when I asked her later what that was all in aid of, she said the whole incident expressed her contempt for men in general and that one in particular. She didn't say it quite as delicately as that."

I sipped at my cappuccino. "And she got the lead in the soap after that?"

"Yes, and that's about when she began to effectively take over her own management, although she let me handle the little details, like getting the contracts drawn up." She looked out at a rich man's launch purring up the creek, but she was seeing the past. There was a freshly bitter quality to her words. They seemed to have been bottled inside and now, shaken up by Bobbi's murder, they were foaming out uncontrollably.

I decided to take advantage of the situation. "She liked women, you said. Did she ever make a pass at you?"

Jennie's brow creased, her eyelids narrowed. "Do I look the type, Dan?"

"No, but neither did Bobbi."

"Point taken. Nobody on the set of *The Empty Gun* was aware of her bent. Not at first, that is. There were rumours, but Bob Melts was smitten with her and tried hard to bed her. He was mightily distraught by her coyness, and eventually became livid enough to attack her verbally on the set. When he learned she preferred females, he seemed to feel personally betrayed."

"How would he know?"

"Maybe Barney O'Malley told him. Barney knows every piece of dirt about everybody on the picture."

"Exactly who is Barney? I've met him but didn't have time to get a fix on him."

Barney, it turned out, was everybody's worst vision of what a movie publicist is. A failed newspaperman, who'd started doing favours for some producers while he was still working for an L.A. paper, getting their stars' names in print, and then just naturally slithering over to the other side of the fence and becoming a dishonest-to-goodness Hollywood flack. Don't fall for his hail-fellow routine, Jennie warned me. Barney was ruthless. His drinking, which she'd heard was always a problem, seemed to get worse on this picture. At one point, everybody assumed he was about to be thrown off the set.

"I've been doing an awful lot of babbling, Dan—not that I haven't enjoyed it, not that I didn't need to talk to someone about all this. But you still haven't offered me anything in return. You conned me into seeing you by saying you had some information for me. So give, guy."

"Well . . . " I said slowly, procrastinating while I could think of something to improvise, "you should be aware of the fact . . . the fact that . . . everyone has been telling me that, aside from Burt Gold, you and you alone were the only key person who was not at the dailies the night of Bobbi's death." Nice going, Dan.

She shivered. "Is that it?" Her voice was taut. "Did anyone tell you that Bob Melts and Peter Cowan were barely there either? That there was three days' worth of film to see and they ducked in and out. And that, according to friends of mine in the crew—like Leo Garnett—Bob and Peter weren't there for a good part of the time? They were both away for an hour or more, at different times. Can we go now? I'm cold."

"No, nobody told me any of that. Let's walk back." Her sudden chill was communicating itself. "I'm really not accusing you of anything, Jennie. The questions go with the job. Believe me." I was almost believing myself. There was something about Jennie that didn't fit my personal, though admittedly uninformed, image of a murderess.

We threaded our way through the market. Once, as a Chinese greengrocer laden with a box of early California corn hove off her port side, I grabbed her gently by the shoulders to pull her to safety. When my hands lingered, she didn't seem to mind.

As we headed up to her place on the slopes, I began asking Jennie questions about herself. She was a small-town girl from New England, who'd travelled the Continent in her early twenties and wound up working for an American filmmaker in London. She made enough contacts to set up a practice as an agent there, and then, homesick, moved to New York and became personal manager for a couple of struggling young actors. She was in a shark-infested profession so she'd had to grow a tough hide. She'd had one great love, never married, and until recently never thought she was missing much. And how about me—married? I told her my story, about Sarah and the kids, and when Jennie asked about my work, I gave it to her whole cloth, embroidering only a little. She listened, clucked in sympathy and laughed at the right moments, and said, summing up, "I prefer men who aren't macho."

At her doorstep, she looked at me with the vulnerability of a mongrel pup in a pet shop. When I embraced her, she shook free but only to find a key in her purse and let us in. I followed her up the stairs. She stopped, turned and leaned into me. She kissed me. I kissed back. Big brothers weren't supposed to feel like this. But little sisters weren't supposed to feel like *that*. We stood there for several minutes, our lips and tongues moving avidly while our hands read our bodies. Then, with the bravado of a high-school football hero clutching a cheerleader, I made the fatal move. My right hand eased up under her sweater and glided towards her bra strap.

Jennie froze, her arms dropping to her side. "No. Dan. I can't."

"Why?" (Oh, God: *Why?*)

Her head hung down, like a rejected pup's. "It . . . It can't go anywhere . . . Anyway, I'm leaving in a few days. Dan, you're a lovely man, even if you're doing a crummy job for a crummy client, but I don't think you'd like the real me. You're just seeing Jeannette Barlow at her weakest, her most feminine. She's not what you think she is."

She lifted her lips to mine for a fleet, final kiss, took my hand and led me to the door. We didn't even say goodbye.

I got home just after the girls did, shouted at Esther for leaving her homework at school, and then at dinner gave her an extra helping of my father's special moist sauerkraut chocolate cake to make up for my misplaced anger.

8

Lady in Waiting

❖❖

Coincidences excite most of us, those little tricks of timing that suddenly loom like fate. They happen occasionally, probably more than we notice. But I figure people who attribute mystical qualities to an accidental conjunction of events probably also believe what they lip-read in *The National Enquirer*. Which is why I was not too impressed with the fact that I just happened to have Georgia West's picture in my pocket as I sat in my car waiting for her outside a Chinatown restaurant. A picture that would let me identify Georgia. A picture that Nadia had couriered to me, by coincidence, just the day before.

Sitting there, a spring drizzle spluttering on my tinny rooftop, I had time to ponder many mundane things. Like the embarrassing literalness of last night's dream: I was a shark trying to catch beautiful small black round fish, but even when I seized one in my jaws their skin proved too strong to penetrate.

Waking up this morning, I'd reached for the cigarettes secreted in the bottom of my bedside dresser and smoked one defiantly. It was Saturday. The girls would be sleeping in. Nobody to tell me that I was violating the sacred smoke-free environment of our home. But I couldn't linger sluglike in bed much longer because I had to get the girls ready to sleep over at Sarah's parents for the weekend.

Over breakfast, Esther and Larissa were curious about what I was doing at the movie studio, wondering when I'd be taking them to meet a real star. They rolled their eyes at one another when I told them we could visit the Planetarium anytime they wanted.

As Esther cleared the dishes, Larissa was down in the basement, sorting the laundry. "Dad! You *didn't*! I told you a hundred times *not to!*"

Oy, Bohz-yeh. What in hell had I done now. Larissa emerged from the netherland, looking as though she'd just seen the Prince of Darkness himself. Arms extended, she bore a white garment, one sleeve hanging from each of her hands. A small white garment. Too small for someone her size.

"This was my *very favourite* Benetton sweatshirt," she said in what surfaced as a wail. "My *all-cotton* sweatshirt. The one I told you a *thousand* times not to put in the dryer. It's ruined."

"Oh, Larissa, I'll get you another one."

"You can't. They don't make them anymore. It was my best one. I was going to wear it to school on Monday." Her face crumpled into tears.

Which was when the Melzers arrived. They'd come to pick up the kids early, as usual. When I let them in, Sarah's mother strode to the kitchen and demanded, "What's the matter, Larissa honey?" Gathering her granddaughter into her expensively clad arms, she glared at me.

On looks alone, Morton and Frieda Melzer wouldn't be your first choice in the character roles of a *Zeda* and *Baba*. Loving grandparents, yes, but at sixty-two Morton was still lean and dapper, a lawyer turned successful developer, and Frieda bespoke elegance. Her hair was not allowed to come out grey, it emerged in sterling silver. With a hallmark. She was not so sophisticated, however, that she refused to pry. After determining that Larissa was not grievously injured, Frieda asked, not so casually, "You're going out this weekend, Daniel?" No, I reassured her, just cleaning the house and working. "Leave the man alone," Morty said, offering me a little male bonding.

A suddenly light-hearted Larissa, shifting with the fickleness of a Pacific wind, made up with me before she left. After they'd all gone, I sat quietly, savouring a cigarette and the silence. Unhurriedly I opened an envelope the courier had dropped off yesterday and Esther had forgotten to tell me about until she was walking out the door. It was a newspaper clipping of the "Today's Smile" photograph of Georgia West, looking like enough of a woman to fool me and the Vancouver *Province* photographer. She was leaning on a wrought-iron rail as black as her long hair. Her lean face did hold hints of Margot Kidder, as Simone had suggested, but a Kidder playing a role more glamorous than Superman's Lois Lane. The text accompanying the colour photo had Georgia's age as 25, her astrology sign Aries, her occupation Model. She liked dressing up, disliked rude men. Only two of the items surprised me: her hobby was writing, she'd said, and her favourite author was Jan Morris, the transsexual travel writer.

I'd called Nadia at home to thank her for the clipping and fill her in about the little I'd learned. Cowan, Georgia West, Breen. Guiltily I avoided any mention of my brief but energetic encounter with Jennie. Not that there was anything between us that should make me feel blameworthy, dammit. But guilt was bred into my Slavic genes, as deeply as the passion for potatoes. Nadia had been intrigued by Graves' continued insistence that someone other than Gold had killed Bobbi Flynn. Let's meet for a late dinner, she'd suggested, scenting another chapter in the Murdered Starlet serial.

❖❖

I'd spent the last half of the morning and well into the afternoon playing at my semi-annual housecleaning. Nature isn't the only one who abhors a vacuum. Wielding a whiny electric broom on automatic pilot, I was really thinking about where I should proceed in the case. The phone had decided for me.

"Dan my man, I got a live one for ya," the pickled-in-lager voice had announced. Mickey, at Kits Cabs. "One of the drivers just called in with a make on that HUSTLE plate you were looking for. The car's down in Chinatown right now. A battered old green Buick, with a bashed-in rear end. And, get this, he saw the driver go into a café. This info is only five minutes old."

"Great work, Mick. Tell the driver I'll bring around his fifty bucks' finder's fee tomorrow."

"Nah, I'll tell him he's getting his twenty-five. I get half for having to deal with this jerk every day."

The Buick was sitting outside the Canchin Café, *Canadian and Chinese Food, Full Breakfast $2.95.* Sure enough, in strolling by, I'd spotted Georgia West in a booth near the back. Now I was waiting in my Mini, hoping to confront her discreetly outdoors, not within the contained universe of the café. I knew it as a joint on Pender in a red-brick building as old as the century. Addicts and hookers hung out here while drug cops viewed all the action through binoculars from an empty room in the building across the street.

What looked like a Hong Kong market street was a humming hive of suburban Canadian Chinese stocking up with the week's provisions. Bok choy, icicle radish, lotus root, monstrous dried mushrooms, leathery shark's fin at forty-eight bucks a pound. In the windows, greasy sausage, dripping soy-sauce chicken, roast duck whose sweetness drifted down a rain-glazed sidewalk that had all but disappeared under hundreds of pairs of feet. In the shops butchers wielded singing stainless-steel cleavers, apportioning barbecued pork, and shoppers shuffled through cramped aisles of what I knew were tacky paper toys and towers of chinaware. The shops spilled over on to the street with bins of vegetables and tubs of seafood.

I had a couple of hours to chronicle the street scene. Both the dank afternoon and I were in decline when Georgia finally stepped out onto Pender in a stylish long raincoat and sky-scraper heels, looking warily around. I waited until she was near her Buick before I got out and called to her, quietly. Her hand froze on the car door. She looked at me frantically, then bolted for a side street a few doors down the block. For a lady in heels, carrying a purse and running in the rain, she galloped along fleetly, like the man she almost used to be. I took after her and, rounding the corner, saw her duck into a back lane. Hot on her high heels, hoping no cop saw this guy chasing a good-looking woman, I followed Georgia down the rain-slick, garbage-strewn alley. Skidding on some discarded mustard greens. Almost tripping on a wooden vegetable crate. But fast as Georgia was, she was having the same problem. I was gradually losing ground when, near the end of the alley, she found the ground face first, after trying to vault a toppled trash can.

Long seconds behind, I managed to grab her by a shoulder pad in her rain coat as she was rising up on one nyloned knee, ready to run again. "Georgia, I'm not going to hurt you," I said. "I just want to talk for a minute. Hold on, for God's sake." She was veering between her female and male selves, trying to slip out of her coat with one arm and winding up to slug me in the head with the other. I grabbed her in a bear hug, pushed her back to the pavement, and straddled her. Luckily, there was no one in the lane to see what looked like a very inept mugging.

"Listen to me," I said in a breathy voice. "My name's Dan Rudnicki, I'm a private detective and I just want to ask you some questions about the Bobbi Flynn case."

71

"Get the hell off me!" Her voice was a deep contralto. "I'm not talking to anyone about anything. I've already talked to the cops. And they got the guy who did it."

I decided to lie. "I know. But Bobbi's family in Des Moines retained me to ask a few basic questions." Maybe mentioning Graves as my client would scare her off. "All they want are a few answers so they can have some piece of mind. Nothing tough. There's money in it for you."

Georgia stopped struggling beneath me. "How much?"

"Fifty bucks for half an hour of your time." There goes the weekend's grocery money.

"All right, all right. Let me up."

She stood, trying to restore some grace as she picked up her purse, straightened her nylons and brushed off her coat. "We can go back to the café." She limped a bit, but lady-like, as we walked up the alley. "Damn it," she said, "you tore my nylon. My knee is bleeding."

We looked a strange pair as we entered the CanChin and headed for a booth in the rear. In any other restaurant, people would have noticed us. Me a rain-drenched runt, still grasping for breath. Her several inches taller, hobbling on spike heels, blood leaking down her leg.

We sat on torn vinyl seats, Georgia with her back to the wall, and ordered coffees from the Chinese waiter. In the unsparing restaurant light, her features seemed slightly more mannish than in her photograph. Yet a long way from a homosexual camping it up in a wig and his sister's clothes. Georgia's cascading hair was her own and the skin on her face had a woman's softness. When she shrugged off her coat, I could see hillocks of breasts rising from the valley of her blouse. She looked more feminine, moved more like a lady, than many women I knew. Jennie and Nadia excepted.

Georgia's first words were "Give me the money."

"You really need it, I hear," I said, going through my wallet and gathering twos, fives and tens to make the fifty. If Adam

Graves was not supposed to be my client, I couldn't tell her I knew he'd given her a large lump sum to stay away from Bobbi Flynn. "More operations?"

Shivering, she draped her coat back over her shoulders. "So you know. You've been talking to someone."

"Just the police."

That seemed to placate her, but she considered before replying, "Mmm, more operations. The puritanical government in this province has stopped paying for any sex-reassignment operations. I have to go to the States to finish things up." She spoke as if she really did read literary Brit authors like Jan Morris.

Slipping the cash into her bulky purse, she said: "You're not going to get much from me for this. I don't know much."

"Georgia, were you with Adam Graves the night of the murder?"

"Yes."

"All night?"

"Most of it. Before, during and after the time she got killed—that's for sure."

Our coffees came. "Did Graves ever leave during that time?"

"Never."

Good, I could trust my client at least that far.

"Did you ever sleep with him, Georgia?" I asked, not trusting him any further than that.

"No. Did anybody say I did?"

"He says you didn't. Just checking. Did he know you were a transsexual?"

She lifted the coffee cup to her lips, cradling it in both hands, studying the crazed walnut veneer of the tabletop as if its network of cracks were fortune-telling lifelines on a palm. "He knew me as a prostitute."

"Did you ever make it with Bobbi Flynn?"

"Who didn't?" Georgia's full lips spread in a thin smile. "She liked being the aggressor with women."

"She was bisexual. Georgia, somebody told me you were complaining, before Bobbi's death, about how hard it was to make it with another transsexual. Who did you mean?"

She reared back instinctively, as if someone was about to hit her. "Who? It's nobody you know. Just another person."

"Another transsexual? It's none of my business, but do you folks tend to hang around with each other?"

My question turned on a spigot and a flood of memory began flowing. "I have a lot of time for people in my condition. Do you know what it's like to be imprisoned in a body that you loathe? No, of course you don't. What's your name? Dan? Ever since I can remember, Dan, I hated being a boy. I knew I was different in kindergarten when I wanted to play with girls ·rather than boys. I enjoyed dressing up in my mother's clothes. I come from a nice middle-class family in the Interior—my father was manager of a sawmill, my mother raised three kids. The other two were 'normal.' My folks were good, conventional role models so in my case it wasn't environment. I don't know, maybe I was born the victim of some medical disorder, like diabetes. Maybe there was some hormonal accident in the womb. There's one psychiatrist in Montreal who says really severe stress in the first part of a pregnancy might upset the production of male hormones in a fetus and that somehow feminizes the brain. Nature, nurture— all I know is that I was a biologically normal person who became convinced that I was a member of the opposite sex. I wanted to have kids, love them, mother them. At university—"

"What did you take?"

"English lit. While I was at university, I learned from a whole series of shrinks that what I had was 'gender dysphoria.' Some of them said I identified with my mother too strongly—blame Mom, isn't that typical?—and they could cure me by encouraging a more appropriate sexual identity. But others said it was too late, my female gender was locked in tight by the time I was eighteen months old. Another shrink told me that I was really a homosexual who was terrified about making love to another male."

I offered her a cigarette, took one myself, trying not to stem the flow. "No, I don't smoke," she said. "It's a filthy male habit. Anyway, whatever the reason, I knew I wanted to *be* a woman. And when I learned about sex reassignment surgery, I knew I would have it performed. I did what the shrinks told me, dressed and lived like a woman for two years. It shocked my family and lost me my job at an advertising agency. I went on welfare, but everything was going along fine until the government decided that it would no longer pay for sex-change operations. That's when I decided I would go on the street."

"Where you met Donny Breen."

Her long sigh sounded like a balloon deflating. "My, we have been a busy little boy, haven't we?"

"Breen: what's he about?"

She stared into her coffee cup before leaning back into the booth and, looking me square in the eyes, said, "Pimping. Violence. Crack. He came on charming and then I saw him when he was sailing on cokc—hc sclls crack, but settles for coke himself. That's bad enough: he was on the stuff the last time he beat me so hard I couldn't hustle for days. But he didn't let me see his true, destructive self until he'd got me some very expensive dates."

"Some of them with Bobbi Flynn."

"One night Donny said he had an interesting trick for me, and took me up to her hotel room. I wasn't crazy about the idea of doing it with a woman—it seemed . . . deviant. But she was insistent, and oh, the money was good. She promised to give me bags more than Donny expected I was getting."

"Did Bobbi know you were a transsexual?"

"Mmm. It seemed to give her a certain perverse pleasure. "

I stopped asking questions for a minute or two and simply gazed at her as I sipped at my dishwater coffee, marvelling at how complete the illusion of her semi-femininity was. In the silence, she stared back as intently, with a quizzical look, as if deciding whether to confide in me. Eventually, she said, "Mr. Detective, I'm scared."

"Of whom? Me? The police?"

"The police? Mmm, the police, Donny—even you. I've been hiding out. How did you find me?"

I told her about the license plate. Georgia smiled, but in embarrassment. It was Breen's sick little idea of a joke, she explained, when he'd given her the old Buick for being a good girl and making him so much money. She could command high fees because she knew how to please a man, with everything short of actual intercourse. She played the seductive female, she said, with a passion that most castrating women don't pretend in these post-feminist times. Yes, it was true as she'd read somewhere, the transsexual is society's most adamant believer in a deep and abiding difference between the sexes. Not only that, she could actually talk intelligently to her tricks after the act.

"You give good head, in both senses," I offered. Then: "Why are you so scared, Georgia?"

"I can't say. But I have to tell somebody in your position, in case something happens. I don't have anyone else like you I can trust. But if you're really working for Bobbi's family, they're the ones who to deserve to know."

"To know what?"

"Never mind for now. I've written it down, so it'll be there if anything more does happen. Here . . ." She trolled through her purse, coming up with the stub of a pencil, and began to write on a serviette. "I'll give you two addresses. This is where I'm staying now. I'm at a girlfriend's. She's out of town. And this is—"

"Hi, Sexpot."

Her head jerked up. Her eyes, looking beyond me, were wide. "Donny!"

I eased the serviette across the table and into my jacket pocket before swivelling around to see a pale-faced, orange-haired pumpkin head atop a tree stump of a torso. A Douglas fir stump. The smile it was smiling was not learned at Dale Carnegie. "Who's this?" Breen asked Georgia, his cool grey eyes flicking my way.

"Dan . . . Nobody. Just a trick, Donny. Go away, Dan, I'm busy now."

Breen's smile was on freeze-frame. He sat down beside Georgia. "Don't leave, Dan. Your last name's not something funny like Roodicky?" His voice was a loud, sibilant whisper. If snakes could speak, they'd sound like his hiss.

"No," I lied, with discretion, not valour. "It's Wright. Dan Wright."

"Yeah? Let's see." He grabbed a lapel of my cord jacket with one hand, then shoved the other into my inside pocket to fish out my wallet. It was a prize catch. "Oh, Rudnicki," he said, reading my licence. "TransWorld Security. Private investigator. Yeah, I heard you were looking for me. And for the Sexpot here. Now you and I are going to talk. You, Sexpot, are going to stay right where you are. I haven't seen you in days. You been avoiding me? Don't try to screw off in your car while I'm talking to this guy. Give me your keys."

She fumbled her purse open and he plucked a keychain from its depths.

"Let's go," he said, dropping my wallet on the table and lifting me up by one shoulder of my jacket. I managed to scoop up the wallet and stuff it in my jacket pocket. Pointing me at the door to the kitchen, he twisted my right arm behind my back in a hammerlock and pushed me through the door, past a surprised but stoic cook stirring a wok, and hustled me outside into the alley.

9

Donnybrook

❖❖

Market Alley was deep in late afternoon gloom, the rain still drooling down. At the far end of the lane, I could see a rubby sifting through a blue dumpster and hear him shouting epithets at nobody, everybody. I could smell the sour vented odours of old Chinese food laced with beer from the pubs that fronted on Hastings. And I could feel the loose gravel on the lumpy pavement beneath my scrabbling feet as Breen propelled me forward, my right arm nearly touching the back of my neck. The exquisite pain turned all my senses on to High. The only thing I could be grateful for was that my life wasn't flashing before my eyes. Yet.

In the next block, forklift trucks were still backing up and down the alley. White-garbed butchers were still unloading what were probably disembowelled pigs' carcasses. Not, I trusted, an omen. In my own little universe, beneath the rows of fire escapes clinging too high above me on the sheer slopes of brick walls, there was no one but the oblivious rubby to witness what might be my oblivion.

Breen marched me into one of the walls, face first, denting more than my pride. "Okay, Sailor, so why the fuck are you screwing around with Georgia?" he demanded, his quiet but crazy voice whistling by me like the wind. He wrenched my arm higher, clockwise.

"Aaah," I muttered between teeth that would soon be gritted down to their gums. I'd better be consistent. "I'm— Hold on! The wing doesn't fold that way! I'm a private detective. Bobbi Flynn's folks hired me."

My forehead hit the wall again. Harder. This time there would be blood. "Bullshit," Breen said. "Who hired you?"

"Her parents."

His knee smashed between my buttocks, crushing my groin into the bricks. "Graves hired you. Why?"

"Right. Graves." So much for consistency.

"Why?"

How much could I tell him? Does loyalty to a client supersede allegiance to your life? Who said "Loyalty is the last refuge of the impractical"? Probably an old Ukrainian saying. "Graves wanted me to hang around the set . . . so the people working on the movie would think he was doing something about Bobbi's murder."

I braced for the next slam or smash.

"So why did he keep you on when they got the guy who offed her?"

"Maybe he didn't believe Burt Gold did it."

"Yeah—who did he say did it?" He lifted my limb until my hand was set at twelve o'clock.

"He didn't."

"So why were you bugging Georgia?"

"Graves thought she may have some ideas about who killed Bobbi. For god's sake, that's all I know. You're wasting your time. I'm dropping the case anyway—it's a dead end." Which could be a prediction of my own fate.

"I don't believe a goddam—" As his searing whisper washed over me, a gravelly voice detonated directly behind us, at full volume: "What the hell you doin', brother!" Breen suddenly let go of me, moving one step away to appear less threatening. He swung around to see the intruder. It was just the rubby from down the lane, expostulating about the universe. I had only a nano-second to consider my saviour, who was peering through the dark with a puzzled expression on his bristly face. I cannonballed past him, exploding like a sprinter out of the starting blocks.

I'd covered a couple of hundred yards of the alley before I made my mistake. I couldn't resist flicking my head back to see where my pursuer was. Breen had pushed the old guy flat on his stomach and was running hard. He moved fast for a Douglas fir. As I looked behind, my feet crashed into what turned out to be a wicker basket, a castaway from a Chinese food store. I went cock-a-hoop, head down on to slimy cobblestones. And landed on the same bleeding spot on my forehead that Breen had bashed into the wall. Looking up through tear-clouded eyes, I saw an open courtyard and the dim shape of a staircase at the back of a building. I pushed myself to my feet and limped quickly to what might be my only chance to attract some help.

The first step was missing. I grabbed at the railing. It was wooden and wobbly. Leaping on to the second riser, I launched my aching self on a series of long flights of ramshackle, slippery stairs that zigzagged their way up the building's three storeys. The staircase swayed in back of me as I reached the top of the first flight. It was Breen, a breath behind. I could hear the rotting wood steps creak in complaint at his heavy body.

Oh-oh. No door on the second floor. Just barred windows, with dirty frosted panes. The next flight of stairs went off to the left. To the right, a corrugated-metal roof. It covered a skinny one-storey shed jutting out like an afterthought from the rear of the building. Strewn about the roof, chunks of metal pipe and cast-off urinals, their porcelain stained with yellow. As I started up the second stairway, Breen grabbed me by one knee and yanked me down. I landed with my backside in a urinal.

The look on Breen's face as he hulked over me was one of fury. His carrot-orange hair was plastered down by the rain, like a demonic halo. Panting, his fat lips gaped open to reveal broken teeth. His eyes were afire with anger. He was like one of the little devils tormenting damned souls that chilled me the time Sarah and I had stared up at the ceiling of the old cathedral in Florence. And if I didn't do something clever, this would be Dan Rudnicki's Judgement Day.

Breen reared back, drew in a rush of air and threw a fist as big and menacing as a mace. Some primitive instinct—which figured my face could suffer no more grievous blows—made me swing my head to the side. His fist just missed. It rammed into the corrugated metal. His yelp was a wounded animal's and he jumped about like a coyote caught in a trap, shaking his torn hand to mute the pain.

Even more enraged, but smart enough a beast to favour his injured paw, he kicked at me instead. His size-14 caught me at the waist. Luckily, it landed between bones. But for sure I wouldn't be modelling underwear for the next few days. Now he was looking madly around the roof for a weapon. I remembered what the guy in Meg's had said: *He grabs whatever's around and uses it as a weapon.* Breen reached down for one of those chunks of pipe.

It was at that point I decided I would no longer be his personal football. Struggling to my feet as he rose back up, I ran at him, leading with a shoulder, trying to feel like a human battering ram. He was obviously caught off guard—hell, it was the first offensive action I'd taken since being marched into the alley. My shoulder met his chest with all the force of my 150 pounds. A flea pummelling an elephant. But the blow contained enough of my suddenly unleashed wrath and sheer desperation to punch the wind out of him. He gasped, and folded in the middle like a jackknife.

Wildly, I leaped down the dozen feet to the rocky courtyard, falling on all fours, tearing my hands and bruising my knees. Just then headlights poked through the dusk of the lane. When the car was a few feet away, moving quickly, I ran in front of it and leaped on the hood. My side hit the metal with a crack that sounded like gunfire and pain sped down my legs and up my spine. The car carried me forward for a few seconds, then the driver—who probably couldn't see where he was going— jammed his brakes. As he stopped, I rolled off the hood. Shouting "Help!", I grabbed at the handle of the back door on the driver's side, swung the door open and flung my battered self inside. "Get moving!" I moaned. The Chinese driver, with a fleeting wide-eyed look back at the lunatic hitchhiker, accelerated out of Market Alley to the comparative safety of the cross street and headed towards Hastings. Which is where he spotted a parked squad car, pulled up beside it, squealed to a stop, leaped out and began semaphoring his arms to the cop behind the wheel just before I passed out.

❖❖

I regained consciousness with my hands up, shielding my face, trying to ward off the next blow from Breen. Instead, someone was shaking me by the shoulder. "Hey, Mac," a voice shouted too loudly into my left ear, "wake up!"

I'm awake, I'm awake, didn't they know I was nearly dying? My eyes were bleary from the blood that had streamed down my forehead, but I could open them wide enough to see the square face of a cop six inches from mine.

❖❖

"I can't smell anything on him," the voice reported.

"The driver says he seemed to be running from someone," a second voice said.

"Okay, help me haul him out."

As large hands began to move me, I resisted and said, "I'm all right. I can get out myself." The hands pulled away and I slowly levered myself from the back seat of the car.

After the two patrol cops decided I would live, the next ten minutes were an undramatic dialogue that established who I was, what I was doing in that condition, when and where it had happened, who had done it, and why. I saw no point in lying about any of it, about Georgia or Breen. With all the battering my head had taken, my brain wasn't bright enough to bend the truth. The only flicker of interest in the boxy-faced cop listlessly interrogating me was when I first mentioned Bobbi Flynn.

"Oh, you're Ranidky," he said.

"Rudnicki."

"Yeah, we got a circular on you from Inspector Rusk. He said you were becoming a pain in the butt on this case. We got Gold locked up in hospital. What the hell does Breen have to do with anything?"

"I wish I knew."

His interest waned as quickly as it had waxed. Did I want to lay an assault charge? Yes—no, I didn't want to spend hours in the cop shop, I wanted to get home. Okay, he'd file a report on the incident, just in case. And he advised me to stop wasting my time trying to unlock an open-and-shut case. Or cruder words to that effect.

My car had a parking ticket wedged under the wiper. Driving home was like doing a decathlon. The final event was the verandah's five-metre flight of steps to the front door. By the time I sank into the safety of my living-room, I was exhausted. Thank God the girls were staying over with their grandparents until tomorrow night. They'd have been shocked to see their old man banged up and torn like the loser in a grudge match between pit bull terriers.

Take an inventory. Forehead caked with blood and throbbing where Breen had bashed it against the wall. Side aching where he'd kicked it and where I'd landed on the hood of the car. Groin sore from being slammed into the brick wall. My knees hurt, my hands were pitted with tiny gravel—the only parts of my anatomy that I didn't feel like amputating were my toes. But, at the moment, the rest of me was not interested in doing any pirouettes.

Shevchenko, sensing I was too weak to slap him away, crawled on to my lap.

I must have sat there, semi-comatose, for an hour or so before the phone began clanging around in my mind like a chorus of bell-ringers tuning up in a belfry. I stood, dumping the cat on the floor, staggered to the phone, fumbled the receiver to my ear and grunted into the mouthpiece.

"I thought we were having dinner," said a voice that could have ushered in the next Ice Age. Nadia. Dinner. Tonight.

"What time is it?" It came out as a croak.

"Too damn late for dinner, Rudnicki." She hesitated. "You sound . . . unwell."

"If that's a euphemism for all banged up and bloody terrified, I guess I'm unwell."

I started to explain lamely, haltingly, about my close encounter with Breen. Before I could finish, she interrupted: "You know what my mother always says, Dan."

I could hardly wait.

"He who goes to bed with dogs wakes up with fleas."

To break the ensuing silence, she asked: "Where are the girls?"

"With Frieda and Morty."

"Well, Florence Nightingale I'm not, Dan, but hold on, I'll be there."

10

Everything I
Wanted to Know

❖❖

Nadia was always there for me. Early this Sunday morning, as I stirred painfully in bed, more of her was *there* than I'd felt in years. I was under the covers, nude. She was on top of them beside me, wrapped in my tatty turquoise robe. And, it appeared, in nothing else.

During the few years I'd had with Sarah, there was always a moment every morning I treasured. The first moment, waking up safe beside another warm loving body, feeling its presence, breathing in its scent. That first moment of consciousness, when life still seemed as simple and fresh as it had when I was a kid.

The next moment, when I moved to wrap my arm around Nadia, I felt like a kid who'd tumbled off his two-wheeler under the wheels of a truck. Everything, from the crown of my head to the caps of my knees, pulsed with pain. Dried blood smeared the pillow where it had seeped through the bandage on my forehead. A bandage. Nadia must have patched me up and put me to bed. Now, still sleeping, she wriggled her bum into my belly. Battered as I was, I computed my blessings. This was the first time in two years we'd shared the same sheets. I decided to take advantage of the situation, if not her. I clasped her *zaftig* body to me, spoon into spoon. Not a good idea, it turned out, because my groin was already aching from last night's bashing.

To distract myself, I began to sift through the confrontations with Breen and Georgia West. Why was she trying so hard to hide? Obviously, her pimp terrified her with his cruelty. But why had Breen been looking for her? Did he want her for more than turning tricks? Georgia had told me two intriguing things. She'd confirmed that she was seeing another transsexual before Bobbi Flynn's death. Was that the slightest bit significant? And what had she meant when she'd said Bobbi's parents "deserved to know"? Know what? Know, maybe, that Breen killed Bobbi? As far as Phil Rusk was concerned, he had his killer safely locked up. But based on my meeting with Breen, Georgia's pimp was supremely capable of violence consummated by murder.

Georgia was on my mind for more than one reason. I'd found her for Adam Graves and lost her, all within one hour. Now I had to locate her again. Sure, Sherlock, how? A tumbler in my mind clicked into place. Of course: the serviette.

I uncoiled from Nadia, removed the covers carefully, and tiptoed out of bed to the cupboard where my dirty cord jacket was neatly hanging. Still stuffed in the pocket was the serviette on which Georgia had scrawled her addresses. Just as I was looking at them, Nadia jerked out of sleep and sat up. "You're a fright, Dan."

My head was swathed in gauze, my knees were scraped and my side bore bruises. Didn't my condition turn her on? No, she muttered, she preferred undamaged goods. Well, I volleyed, she could restore them to their original virginal condition with a little loving care. With what I seemed to have in mind, she returned, I would no longer be a virgin. Her point. My hopes rose for a return match—with live action—when she asked how I felt, I told her, and she ordered me back into bed. But as I snuggled in, she rolled smoothly out and said she'd be back with some breakfast.

Ten minutes later, she brought in a bed tray of scrambled eggs and toast for two. We sat munching, Nadia safely on the big wicker chair across the room, while I gave her more details about my jousts with Georgia and her pimp. As I talked, something profound occurred. The more I remembered about the fight with Breen, the more angered I became about what had happened. By the time I finished the story, I was enraged about what had almost happened.

"I'm convinced that sunuvabitch was prepared to kill me, Nadge. He would have *relished* doing it. And if he didn't actually murder Bobbi, I bet my brother-in-law's life savings Breen had a hand in it somehow. He's got Georgia paralyzed with fear. She wanted to tell me something, and she may have if he hadn't shown up. She's an intelligent, thoughtful human being, whatever sex she is . . . I've got two addresses where she stays and I'm going to follow up with her."

"Dan, why don't you just lay an assault charge against Breen and let the police do all the dirty work?"

"I just might, but I'm being paid to locate Georgia. The police have no reason to find her for me. More to the point, I feel like Pinocchio. I'm being jerked around like a puppet, my nose is out of joint, and I'm not the one who's doing the lying. I don't know if anyone's told me the truth so far—except maybe Georgia." What I didn't say, because I may not have realized it then, was that Donny Breen had challenged me at some deep wellspring of my manhood. Did I know at the time I was looking for revenge? I should have known that, in this case, *living* was the best revenge.

Nadia, brave about her own life, was a coward about mine. "*Zarozamili* — go, get yourself killed. You, you're . . . *prosti hlop.*"

If I recalled my Ukrainian-school lessons correctly, she was telling me that I was a know-it-all ignoramus. One thing I knew for sure: she was upset.

As she gathered her clothes together and flounced out to get dressed, she said, "Goodbye, I'm leaving, but you're not going anywhere today. You're staying in bed until dinner and then you're taking the kids over to your brother's place. It's Easter, remember?"

I hadn't remembered. But Nadia kept a watching brief on me, from a distance, and knew the girls and I always went to Myron's for a traditional Ukrainian Easter dinner. I fell asleep while visions of *paska* and *pysanky* danced in my head.

Why is it you can have a hard time finding friends but can never lose relatives? Families are forever. No matter how you may try to disown your kin, they inhabit your very veins. And while blood may be thicker than water, it's a lot messier.

As Myron opened the door to us that evening, the sweet scent of freshly baked loaves of *paska* greeted us along with his basso profundo "*Hrystos Voskres!*" Christ is risen.

Esther and Larissa chorused the ritualistic reply: "*Voistynu Voskres!*" He sure has.

My brother-in-law the doctor, staring with professional interest at my bandaged forehead, was about to remark on it when my sister bustled into the hall. Wiping floury hands on her apron, warm, round Rose cried "*Moi mali divchata!*" and gathered her little girls in her arms. Then she saw the bandage and said, "What happened to your father's head?"

"I fell off my bike," I said, repeating the lie I'd told Morty and Frieda when they brought the kids home.

"And you were not wearing a helmet, I am positive of that," Myron tsked, adopting the professorial tone he'd taken with me the moment he began dating my sister. The fact that my wand-thin brother-in-law had high blood pressure and an ulcer never stopped him from lecturing me about my lifestyle. It didn't help that he was one of the better surgeons in town and I was still trying to decide what I wanted to be if I grew up.

Fortunately, my kids got on better with his slightly older son and daughter. They were awaiting us with their grandfather in the expansive, expensive living room of Myron's rambling Shaughnessy manse, all leaded windows and dark-oak paneling. The place was polished and shiny from the spring cleaning a lot of Ukrainian Canadian women must do before Easter.

My father stood up to greet us. "*Yak schimyish,*" he said formally, holding out his hand as if he didn't see me every second day.

"And how are you, *stary dyeed,*" I said. Calling him "old man" was one way of telling him to relax, even if he was in Myron's perfectly preserved castle.

"You're late, Danylo," my brother-in-law announced. "No time for a before-dinner drink. Rose wants us all at the table."

We sat down, the eight of us, to a diningroom table adorned with silver-headed pussy willows and bowls of Rose's *pysanky,* the hollow Easter eggs she painstakingly decorated like miniature mosaics. My sister was a good enough artist to sell her eggs throughout the year. Myron, seeing me eye them, said, "Those were blessed at church this morning. Where I did not see you or the girls."

"Well, that makes twenty years in a row I've missed the Easter service," I said.

Larissa flashed me a daughter's look that said: *Don't start, Dad.* "Everything smells majorly wicked, Aunt Rose," she said quickly.

"I take it that this is a *compliment,* Larissa," Myron said. You could hear the italics when he spoke.

"Oh, sure, it means the same thing as 'fully rad,'" she said as all four kids stifled smirks.

My turn to leap in. "It all does look wonderful, Rose." She'd brought in a platter of crisp-skinned pork, the stripped-down equivalent of the traditional suckling pig that would have grossed out the children. Amid jokey chatter, we passed plates of ham, pork, garlic sausage, cabbage rolls, sliced beets, three kinds of salad, horseradish relish, cottage-cheese cake, and a cold meat loaf called *saltsesson* which the kids didn't know was made from the kidneys, hearts, tongues and ears of pigs.

Myron proposed a toast to the missing relatives, my brother and his family in Winnipeg. I held up my glass of syrupy white wine in a salute to the chef, who beamed. As always, Rose asked me if I was seeing anybody special these days. I thought of Jennie before shaking my head wistfully. My father entertained us, as he usually did at family gatherings, with stories of how feast days were celebrated in the Old Country. "It's a good thing for you girls that the boys don't throw water on you the way they used to on Easter Monday in the old days." All this talk of Ukraine led my brother-in-law into a dissertation on how the nationalist movement was finally surfacing in that Soviet republic, with its sorry history of subjugation. Our offspring listened respectfully long enough before sidetracking the conversation to the latest Russian rock star making his North American debut. From there, things fell apart as we feasted on an apricot-stuffed layer cake with an unpronounceable name.

After coffee and liqueurs, the group dissolved. The kids helped clean up, then went to play computer games. My father convinced his daughter to return to the kitchen and run through the recipes for her apricot cake and the, uh, pig loaf. That left Myron and me, alone. "So, Danylo," he said uneasily, "and how is that *job* of yours?" There was a family compact not to tell him anything too upsetting about my lifestyle. Somehow he'd been left with the impression, which Rose reinforced, that I was an executive or at least a manager at TransWorld Security.

"Good," I lied. "Things are good."

The silence between us shrieked.

"Well, then," he said at last, warming up with another shot of Bailey's Irish Cream, "any interesting cases?"

"Funny you should ask," I replied, immediately recognizing an opportunity to actually capitalize on a conversation with my brother-in-law. "We have this intriguing case involving a transsexual."

"Male to female?"

"Of course. Isn't that the norm?"

"Oh certainly, but roughly one in six operations is female to male. Going the *other* way is a much less complicated operation."

"Have you ever done a sex change, Myron?"

"That's a *plastic* surgeon's job, and they prefer to call it *altering*. It's merely altering a person's appearance because true sex involves a multitude of factors, such as anatomy, biology, endocrines, cell structure—this cannot be changed. No, I have *not* performed one, but I *do have* a colleague in Calgary who's done many of them, and I *have* attended seminars on the topic, out of mere interest. I find it personally *distasteful*—as do most plastic surgeons in Canada these days."

"Why?"

"I regard it as *mutilation*."

"No matter how you slice it?" Either he ignored my jest or didn't get it. I soldiered on: "How is it done, the male-to-female operation?"

Leaning back, loosening his tie, he was in Myron heaven. He'd been invited to elucidate a complex medical topic, on which he was the resident expert. And he had a captive audience of one, who happened to be his typically less-informed brother-in-law.

"We have been able to do it, surgically, since the early 1930s." (Who asked for a history lesson?) "The first surgeon to

❖❖

attempt it was a German." (Why was I not surprised?) "But the technique was never really *refined* until the Fifties. You remember Christine Jorgensen in Denmark, of course. Then about the mid-Sixties Johns Hopkins opened a gender identity clinic in Baltimore, and that gave the whole transsexual movement a *respectability.* More recently, there was that transsexual tennis player, Renee Richards."

"Fascinating, Myron, but how do you do it?"

"I'm *coming* to that. Your sister tells me you always were impatient, Danylo, ever since you were two weeks premature. The physical side of it is *relatively* simple, really, even though it does demand the combined services of a urologist, a gynecologist and a plastic surgeon. Behind the male sex organs there lies a natural cavity, between the prostate and the rectum. After a penectomy and a bilateral orchidectomy—"

"Meaning?

"*Castration.* After the penis and testicles are removed, the team performs a *vaginoplasty,* replacing them with skin grafts to fashion an artificial vagina. Naturally, for as much as a year, the patient must wear a rubber insert to prevent the grafts from shrinking closed."

"Naturally. Can they feel any sensation in that phony vagina?"

"Generally, yes. The skin graft, if I recall, is usually taken from the buttocks area and some penile or scrotal skin is used, so orgasmic sensation is usually quite possible."

"What about breasts?"

"In fact, they get female hormones, estrogen and progesterone, for a long time before the operation. This tends to develop the breast area *somewhat,* along with reducing bodily hair and softening the skin. But the breasts routinely need *augmentation,* most often with inserted implants. And this is followed by more estrogen therapy. Unfortunately, from what I've heard, it does *not* always end there. Some transsexuals

94

want their ears tucked in, their jaw cut back, even have their thyroid cartilage—their Adam's apple—removed . . . "

"And you said the whole process for female to male is even more complicated?"

Oh, heavens yes, Myron sniffed, pouring himself another slug of Bailey's. Women had to take androgen to stop menstruating, get facial hair growing, maybe even lower the voice a little. Testosterone could reduce the size of the breasts a bit and enlarge the clitoris, which helped later, as he would explain. *Unfortunately,* he said, shaking his head, the male hormones could have some long-term side effects, such as bouts of pimples and an increase in the sex drive that was not always welcome at the time. Surgery on a woman began with a bilateral mastectomy—removal of the breasts, then the womb and the ovaries. The vagina did survive. Myron's colleague had told him that not all female-to-male transsexuals wanted a phony phallus. But for those who did, a surgeon often built one by cutting a flap of skin from the abdomen and forming it into a tube—meanwhile, closing up the vagina. Sometimes this jerry-built penis could urinate, but sometimes the doctor left the woman's uretha where it was, below the penis. After the operation, the patient may have felt like a new man, but he still had to sit down to pee. And—worst of all, as far as I was concerned—he felt absolutely no sexual sensation down there and couldn't have an erection without the help of a prosthetic implant.

"Enough, Myron," I said, as he began to describe the rod-like stiffener that ran through the manufactured penis and could sometimes put pressure on the clitoris and induce an orgasm. "I'm really only interested in the male-to-female variety. You've laid out enough gory detail to give me dry dreams for a week."

With impeccable timing, Larissa wandered in to the living room. "What gory details, Uncle Myron? Tell me all of them!"

Her uncle began turning as red as the sliced beets we'd devoured at dinner. He was never comfortable around sex outside of the operating room, and certainly not in the presence of a precocious thirteen-year-old niece.

"The goriest detail is that it's eleven o'clock," I said, saving him, "and you kids are off to music camp tomorrow."

Her groan built into a chorus when her sister learned of my treachery. They couldn't leave. My father had been playing Wheel of Fortune with his grandchildren on the computer, and winning. "We're going—now," I told the girls. With a hug from Rose and a handshake from Myron, we left only thirty-five minutes after my final ultimatum.

11

Handing Me
a Line

❖❖

My favourite animal is the chameleon. I identify with that Old World lizard. It can move each eye independently, which would be a handy trait for a detective. To zap food, it has a sticky tongue, which is longer and more lethal than William F. Buckley's. Its toes work like tongs, which give it a firmer perch on life than I have. But most of all, it can transform itself to match its surroundings—and that's the characteristic I covet most. This Easter-Monday afternoon, for instance, I wanted to be a doctor. I was going to be a doctor. I wanted to breach the locked and guarded confines of Riverview, the mental hospital where Burt Gold was being held, still not formally charged with murder. If he was sedated, and in a closed ward, there should be no police guard to talk my way past.

I'd woken that morning feeling pummelled and pained, yet determined to track down Georgia. Graves was right: Georgia could answer more questions than I'd had a chance to put to her the other night. And her answers might help unravel the mystery of who killed Bobbi, if Burt Gold hadn't. More to the point, I was worried about Georgia. Where was she? Had she managed to escape from Breen? I was just as worried about me. What if Breen came stalking the private investigator pursuing the case? What if he found out I had a couple of kids?

Fortunately, the girls were spending Easter week working on their piano and violin at a music camp on Bowen Island, just outside Vancouver. Just because I preferred country music was no reason they shouldn't appreciate the classics. I had packed them up and sent them off with their trusty grandfather, who was squiring them to the ferry. With Shevchenko fed, I'd driven into the East End, to the two addresses Georgia had written on the serviette. One was a respectable aluminum-sided bungalow, the other a rundown wooden two-storey. No one home. I'd hung around each place for half an hour or so before deciding to come back again another time. Today I would talk to Gold.

One thing you learn at TransWorld is how to be a human chameleon. They don't exactly tell you to lie, but they do show you how to work plastic—how people doctor credit cards and driver's licences to give themselves a new identity. As a doctor, perhaps. The rationale is not that you should commit this illegal act yourself, you should merely be aware of how others do it. Sure.

What you do—what I did a while ago—was order another driver's licence from the government. I really thought I had lost mine, but it was only mislaid, and reappeared a few weeks after I'd received its replacement. Now I had two licences. Using a word-processing program on a computer, I printed out a new name and address in little block letters that looked like the government's type style. RUTRICK, DR. DON was close enough to RUDNICKI, DAN that it matched my scrawled signature at the bottom of the licence. I carefully pasted this new strip of skin-thin but opaque paper over the old identification and paid an unscrupulous acquaintance at a laminating place to re-seal the licence with another layer of plastic. Only a cop would notice that there's no blue sky the way there should be behind the name and address. And only the most informed mind would know that most doctors don't like to advertise their title on their driver's licence.

I never use my licence for very nefarious purposes. It comes in handy on those jobs where I need whatever respectability the medical establishment can lend me. Like this Easter Monday, as I drove under heavy-lidded skies into Riverview.

The hospital overlooks the Fraser but doesn't quite have a view of the river flowing through the suburb of Coquitlam on its meander to the sea. If patients aren't depressed before they get here, they soon will be. The government keeps threatening to close down this sprawling citadel of cheerless red-brick buildings with barred windows which dates back before the turn of the century. Centre Lawn Unit is the five-storey building where the hard cases come. It's newer but only slightly more inviting, despite a lawn dotted with picnic benches and a couple of luxuriant weeping willows. *Acute Assessment and Treatment Program*, says the sign at the foot of a long flight of stairs leading to its ominous, columned entrance. Inside, even though the hallway is lined with soothing reproductions of English cottages and roses, it still smacks of Mental Institution.

So did the fierce middle-aged woman behind the plexiglass at the information desk. When I said I'd like to see Burt Gold, her skinny eyes narrowed even more. "Are you a relative?"

Hell, and I'd gone to the trouble of putting on my all-purpose black pinstripe suit to make me look reputable. In wordless reply, I pulled out my driver's licence and poked it through the hole in the glass long enough for her to spot the medical title but not the missing sky. "Oh, Doctor, I'm sorry," she said, retrenching. "Is he a patient of yours?"

"I work for the film company. I'm doing an evaluation."

"Well, you'll have to see our Dr. Eton first. Mr. Gold is in one of our closed wards, of course, and you'll need formal permission to see him."

What I was afraid of. "Certainly. Is Dr. Eton available?"

She'd check. It took her two minutes on the phone to learn that, by coincidence, he was on his way over here. As she hung up, Dr. Eton came in the door. Tall, spare-looking, he had long, hollow-cheeked features that could have been plucked from an early Picasso. An administrator who was, I hoped, too busy with the problems of running an antiquated mental hospital to worry about credentials.

"Dr. Eton, there's a doctor—a Dr . . . uh?"

"Rutrick," I said helpfully, extending my hand to Eton, who took it reflexively.

"He wants to see Mr. Gold, the man from the movie company. On D-4."

"Oh yes," Eton said in a strained voice as thin as his face. "Have you been treating him?"

"Actually, no, but I represent the film company, and naturally we'd like to have our own evaluation of the situation. I'd appreciate seeing him for a few minutes, if possible."

"Well, I'm just on my way to observe another patient. I can give you a quick review of the case. Then, if you still would like to see him, that can be arranged. Rutrick, did you say? Psychiatrist?"

"No, you might say mine is a general practice, but I've been on call recently to the movie studio in West Vancouver."

"Ah. Right. Well, the case is a bit of a puzzle, I'm afraid," Eton said, pressing the button for the elevator. A man in a hurry, he summarized as we took the elevator to the fourth floor. "He came in exhibiting extreme behaviour. Classic symptoms. Paranoia, memory loss, depression. Hallucinations, anxiety over people spying on him, sending secret messages in the newspaper. That sort of thing. Now, our people say he's not truly psychotic. Speaking personally—at this point, I'd never say this publicly—your man doesn't seem the killer type. Claims he didn't do it, not surprisingly. Certainly he's displayed no signs of violent behaviour, no assaultiveness since the first day or so.

"I'm truly puzzled at how he broke down to the point where he'd be capable of murder. The only background we've been able to determine—from people who knew him—is that he'd been depressed for some time. Something to do with how his work was going at the studio. Surprisingly, he'd been sleeping well, we gather. Although that's no longer true. We had to put him in a single bedroom because he hasn't been sleeping through the night since he came here. Strange, all in all. We suspect he'd been on a prescription drug of some sort. Haven't been able to determine what, if any. Nobody we've interviewed at the movie studio claims to know anything about his being on medication."

"Who've you talked to there?"

"The head man, I gather. Graves, is that it? And their publicity fellow, who seemed more concerned with keeping things out of the press. One or two others. An Englishman—the director of the picture, if I remember. And a woman who called to see about his condition. She had some connection with the dead woman."

"Jennie Barlow? Her agent?"

"That sounds right. She was the one who told us he'd been sleeping well. In any case, we've tried to keep the patient off all but the mildest tranquillizers. Bit of an experiment. But I can assure you we're monitoring it hour by hour. The paranoia seems to be settling down. We're getting clearer statements from him. Mind you, he still often talks in riddles. Here we are."

We were at the locked doors to D-4. He buzzed, and a young woman in street clothes let us in. A nurse, it turned out. In this ward, you could tell the patients by the fact that most of them were in bathrobes and pyjamas. "It's co-educational, as you can see," Eton said quietly, gesturing to a lounge he called the day room. "Most of the people here are unpredictable, but we control the worst actors with phenothiazines and the like." Some of the men and women were watching television, others doing jigsaw puzzles, a few playing billiards. It was calmer than I'd expected, except for a dim moaning in the background like the muffled lowing of a cow. One man of indeterminate age stood at a rigid forty-five-degree angle, his arms splayed—a windmill's blades. A couple of elderly women patients paid particular attention to us. One in a housecoat walked up and invaded my personal comfort zone. She stared me in the face with Orphan Annie eyes and then shook her head as she shuffled away in slippers. Probably not cute enough for her.

"What more can I tell you?" Eton wanted to know.

I explained this was just a routine visit, I was sure Burt Gold was getting the best of care, I merely had to satisfy my employers he was stable. Anxious to move on to his waiting patient, Dr. Eton shook my hand and smoothly delivered me to a social worker on the ward. A slight redhead, she looked too vulnerable to be working behind locked doors. But Connie navigated me through the patients—stopping to pat one here, listen to one there—with the aplomb of a Cunard captain.

"Burt, you have a visitor," she announced as we entered a narrow private room. Just space enough for a kid-sized desk, a stacking chair and the bed a pyjama'd Burt Gold was perched on. He seemed even skinnier and a lot less scary than when he'd exploded into Adam Graves' office waving a gun. His eyes —the last time I'd seen them, they were wide open behind granny glasses—were now slumberous. His crown of black curls was matted and stringy. He worked up a weak smile for the vivacious Connie, who introduced me as Dr. Rutrick and left us to talk.

He didn't seem to recognize me. "Burt, how are you?"

No answer. He shifted on the bed, gazed out the window. The seconds multiplied into minutes. I cleared my throat a couple of times. "Burt?"

Without turning to look at me, he finally began to talk. The voice was faraway. "How am I? *Who* am I? I don't know who I am anymore. I don't know what I remember and what I've been told I remember. What is real? Am I?"

Those lines sounded awfully familiar. I decided to try shock therapy. "Burt, what happened? Why did you come in with the gun and threaten Adam Graves?"

"A man needs a little madness, or else . . . he never dares cut the rope and be free."

Oh yeah. Play his game: "Maybe you had every right to be a little crazy, Burt."

"I do *here*. You walk in, and right away they say you're crazy —and then they start sticking things in your arm. I mean, how do they expect to see you get uncrazy if you—you're asleep all the time?"

"Is that why you're staying awake?" Wait a minute. I remembered his last little speech. From a movie I'd rented more than once. Right, *Dog Day Afternoon.* And no wonder I knew the first words he'd spoken: An old late-night favourite, Ingrid Bergman in *Anastasia.* But "a man needs a little madness"—I couldn't place that line. Maybe this was how Burt Gold the screenwriter was escaping reality. Taking refuge in comforting and strangely appropriate lines from some of the great old films. Films he must have known virtually by heart. Either that or he was playing parlor games with me.

Two could play. My video addiction might finally pay off. "I don't think you're guilty, Burt. A guy like you shouldn't be allowed to get in here in the first place. I know that. And I hate to stand here and try your patience like this, but either I'm dead right or I'm crazy."

"You wouldn't care to put that to a vote, would you, Senator?"

Bingo. I'd improvised on Jimmy Stewart's classic Senate filibuster in *Mr. Smith Goes To Washington.* And Gold had come back crisply with the other senator's challenge. Well, this could be fun—I love old movies too—but it sure as hell wasn't getting me any answers. "Burt, let's stop doing Hollywood dialogue. I think I can help. I really don't believe you're guilty of anything but going off the deep end. You didn't kill anybody. You couldn't kill anybody, could you?"

"Don't tell me I'm innocent, Carlo. I know what I did."

"Oh for God's sake," I said, raising my voice for the first time, "you are not Al Pacino and we are not re-making *The Godfather*." Time to get serious. "Now listen up," I said in my best John Wayne, "where *were* you when Bobbi Flynn was killed?"

That shook him. His head fell down into his hands and he started sobbing. "Bobbi, Bobbi. She was so beautiful. Why was she so ugly to me?"

A male patient passing by looked in at the weeping man, then moved on hurriedly.

"Did you kill her, Burt?"

"No!" The reply came so abruptly it startled me.

"Can you prove it?"

"I don't—I can't—I don't know."

"Where were you when Bobbi was murdered?"

He clutched his face again and his body rocked from side to side. "I wasn't there. I was with *him*. Watching him drinking . . . getting drunk."

"With whom?"

"Him. That fat disgusting old man." And in a different, deeper voice: "*Well, come see a fat old man sometime!*"

I was losing him. That sounded suspiciously like Wayne in *True Grit*. I might be one step away from establishing Gold's alibi. "Which fat old man, Burt? What's his name?"

"O'Malley. Bastard O'Malley."

"What were you two doing—"

"How are you doing, Burt?" It was Connie. The smiling social worker came in, looked askance at me and held Gold by the shoulders. "Are you upset? Perhaps he's had enough for today, doctor. Are you tired, Burt?"

"So tired."

Connie nodded me out of the room, then followed a minute later. We shouldn't exhaust him, she said. He was very slowly improving, even though he did lapse into strange speech patterns at times. She found it helpful when I explained that it was vintage movie dialogue and quoted some samples from my interview with Gold. She smiled and we strolled to her office, where she poured me a coffee and, with her permission, I lit up a long-overdue cigarette.

"Do you think he's a murderer?" I asked Connie.

"I really—" She withdrew her immediate response and thought for a moment. "My professional answer is that—well, from the brief time we've had to assess him, I really don't know. My personal one is: I doubt it. And you?"

"I think he just gave me an alibi, but I'm not sure it's one the police will buy. He probably offered it to them already and they've rejected it for good reason."

"What was it?"

On the night of the murder, I said, he was supposedly with a drunken Barney O'Malley. She interrupted when I began to describe O'Malley. "I know who he is. I talked to him on the phone. He was a bit of a pig. I hope he's not a friend of yours."

"Not a chance. A pig, how?"

Apparently O'Malley was not only concerned with making sure that Riverview didn't offer any details to the press. He was also suggesting they keep Gold well sedated and under heavy guard—he was a terrifically dangerous man. O'Malley was particularly interested in knowing which drugs they'd be putting their patient on. When Connie said the hospital had ample security precautions and didn't need any medical advice, thank you, O'Malley swore at her. She wouldn't tell me what he said. But she was sure he was drunk—and how did a drunk manage to survive as a publicity man for a movie?

"A good question. In the old days, it seemed to come with the territory, but I've been told the modern publicist is a heckuva lot more professional. Anyway, it's a question many people on the set have been asking. From what I can see, everybody tolerates O'Malley . . . Incidentally, Dr. Eliot mentioned that Jennie Barlow and Robert Melts called about Burt."

She said the hospital hadn't been able to reach any of Gold's relatives in California quickly, so they'd relied on the movie people for information. Jennie had called on her own and was helpful about his recent condition. There was another call from her only this morning to say she'd arranged to have a local lawyer represent Burt. "Nice woman," the social worker said, and I nodded in agreement, trying not to look rueful.

To learn more about Burt, Connie had contacted Melts and met him briefly at his hotel. The director had been cool, but she sensed an underlying anger, even a rage about the situation. She didn't know which upset him more: that Burt had allegedly killed Bobbi—for whom he professed more than professional interest—or that the murder had disrupted his picture. Did I know Melts well? Barely, I said. Well, how about Adam Graves?

We traded stories about Graves for a while. In her brief interview with him in his office, he had tried to come on to her. "I find him terrifically macho," she said. "And, frankly, I don't mean that in a positive way. He's almost a parody of what I used to read about the typical Hollywood producers. He sures loves his women."

"That's a side of him I haven't seen yet."

"Well, doctor, it sounds like being a medical consultant on a movie set is a very interesting position," Connie said, rising to conclude our little talk.

"Please, don't call me doctor. It's Dan. *Don.*"

She raised her russet eyebrows but didn't pursue my split personality. Leading me out, she stopped to check on Gold. I leaned in and said, "I think you're getting good care here, Burt. Good luck."

Smiling a secret smile, he mumbled a reply. I thought it sounded like: "Oh, these are still halcyon days." That could have been a quotation too, but from Shakespeare—a character in one of the Henry plays, talking about a period of unseasonable calm. Maybe there was a screen version. But unless I was mistaken, nobody ever made a movie of *Henry VI, Part I.*

❖❖

12

Bloody
Hell

❖❖

As my Mini slogged into a misty East End, k.d. lang was crying that tears don't care who cry them. The mournful skies of Easter Monday had wept overnight in a seasonable storm. Today, the stubborn last teardrops of rain were pelleting the windshield just often enough to give my tired wipers a workout they didn't need. My mood was as dampened as this mid-April morning. It wasn't helped by having to drive through the lowest-rent side of town, where too many exhausted houses huddle on too many meagre lots. Vancouver, minus its suburbs, is a sliver of a city squeezed between mountain and sea. There never seems to be legroom enough for all the other Canadians and the immigrants who want a piece of it. Most of the newcomers alight in the East End, hoping it's their only way station on an express train to Nirvana.

Lighten up, Rudnicki. Can the pop sociology. Anyway, it was all sour grapes. The East Side has more tangy ethnic juice, its people have more natural effervescence in a single block than in the whole of the bland, bubble-less West Side.

Could I be missing the kids already? Was I feeling frustrated at another stop in the sack by Nadia, especially after my rebuff from Jennie? Did confronting a mind-blown Burt Gold make me wonder if I'd ever unsnarl this case? All of the above. But probably my biggest worry was Breen and what he might have done to Georgia West. I'd gone to the downtown library and looked through the *Criss-Cross* directory to find the occupants' names and phone numbers for the addresses she'd given me. One was listed as vacant and phoneless, the other housed a D. Martini, who didn't answer. Which was why I was making a return visit to both places, this time determined to look inside.

The closer one stood on a street of small but tidily tended houses. Flanking some of their gates were plaster statues, rip-offs of antique Roman vases and rampant lions, strongly suggesting an immigrant Italian influence. This statueless bungalow had white aluminum siding and a front yard pink with the petals of a flowering cherry tree. At first there was no response to my repeated knocking on the front door. But with the superior peripheral vision of the trained detective, I saw a shape peeping from behind lace curtains—man or woman, I couldn't tell. I stepped back on to the sidewalk and into the rain to give the peeper a full frontal. When I went back to rapping, a faint "What d'you want?" filtered through the door.

"I'm looking for Georgia West. She gave me this address the other night. She wanted me to have it just in case something happened. I think something may have happened."

"Are you the—the private detective?"

"That's me. Dan Rudnicki. Can we talk?"

"Show me some proof."

I pulled out my wallet, extracted my investigator's licence and slid it through the mail slot. A couple of minutes passed. Maybe the dude was dyslexic.

Then a snap of a lock and slowly the door eased open to the length of a chain. I still couldn't tell whether it was a man or a woman. The face that met mine fell into some limbo between. It had shoulder-length black hair but a square male jaw. No facial hair but skin that was scarred and inflamed. Black skirt and sweater over a bulky body. The feet, shod in women's sandals, were man-sized and shaggy.

"Are you alone?" a deep voice asked.

"Only me and my shadow. Which I can't see in this rain. Are you Martini?"

"Yeah, Daniela Martini."

Damned if she didn't look more like a Daniel to me. "Well, you probably noticed on my licence that my given name is Danylo, so maybe we have something in common," I cracked.

"I doubt it. C'min." Unlatch of chain.

I stepped right into the livingroom of a house that was as schizophrenic as its inhabitant. The frilly lace curtains contrasted with the mannish black vinyl sofa. A pot of narcissus perched on a rough brick-and-boards coffee table. Copies of *Vogue* rubbed shoulders with *Road and Truck*.

"Daniela, I'll get to the point. I'm worried about Georgia. I guess she told you we met the other night and she gave me two addresses where I could reach her—this is one of them. Is she here?"

"No, but I'm not tellin' you where she is until you tell me why you wanna see her."

"A couple of reasons. One is outright selfish. I'm investigating Bobbi Flynn's murder even though the cops think they have the guy who did it. The other reason is that I think Donny Breen might do some major harm to Georgia, and I hope that I can get her some protection." A genuine hope, even if it hadn't crystallized until that moment.

"I *know* Breen is after her. And Georgia's nearly pukin', she's so scared. But she's bloody angry too."

"What's your connection with her?"

"We're—we—we've been goin' through the same things."

"You're a transsexual?"

"Well . . . yeah. Gettin' there."

I decided to let him talk me into his confidence. He was still a he, as it turned out. We sat across the coffee table, and it didn't take much prodding to convince him to tell me that he and Georgia had been friends for the last two years as Daniel tried to become Daniela. His buddy was much further advanced in her operations. Yeah, he'd taken the hormone therapy, let his hair grow long, and had been trying to live as a woman. But with much less success, given his build and heavily masculine features. Not to mention his lingering male speech patterns, I thought. The scars and red welts on his face were from depilation treatments—electrolysis to remove his beard—that were done too fast and went badly wrong. And then he was caught financially when the provincial government's health plan suddenly announced no more payments for sex-change operations.

"Those bastards say it's just cosmetic surgery. And for me to get a vaginoplasty will cost me nearly five thousand bucks. Which I don't got, friend. You try livin' half-way as a woman, try gettin' a job. I love kids but d'you think anybody will hire me to work with them." It wasn't a question. "My family, what's left of them, don't wanna know me. Only my mother cared about what's happenin' to me—she left this house to me in her will. Georgia is the only one now that understands. And I'm tryin' to help her. Made her stay with me the last few days. To protect her from that goddam Breen."

"We're in this together then," I said. "Why not take me to where she is?"

His wrecked face crumbled. His eyes teared. "I told her not to go anywhere. I went out to get some food at the Chinaman's. And when I got back, there was this note on the table. Said she *had* to get her diary where she hid it at her place."

"What makes the diary so important?"

"She wouldn't tell me. Just said she wanted me to have it in case somethin' happened to her."

"Why didn't she wait and let you go and get it? Or ask you to go with her for protection?"

"Read the note," he said, pushing it across the cedar slab of the table.

Daniela—I'm going to get the diary I told you about, Georgia had written. *Don't worry, I'll be back soon. I know you warned me not to go anywhere without you. But I'm tired of living like a trapped animal. You of all people understand how frightened I am, Daniela, but if I let Donny Breen make me a captive in my own life, he's won —just as if he had killed me. I'm doing this as a little declaration of my own independence. The test of courage is not to die but to live. —Love, G.*

I think I recognized that last manifesto from my third-year Italian drama course. Georgia's note was a strange blend of bravado and true bravery. She was a complex, courageous, literate, lovely—and, given the circumstances—stupid person.

"Is she at this other address she gave me?" I said, showing Daniela the scrawl on the serviette. "I'll go and bring her back."

"That's her place. She just moved into the dump a couple of months ago when she was tryin' to get away from Breen. I'll come with you."

"No, you stay here in case she comes back before I get there. She'll be upset if she finds you gone. Now, where's she hidden the diary?"

After sputtering in argument, he agreed to hold tight. "I'm not sure where the damn thing is. But a few weeks ago, I caught her kneelin' down in front of her fireplace. Her hands were black as coal and she looked goddam scared that I'd seen her there. She got up real fast and pretended she was just cleanin' things up."

I went to leave.

"Hey!" he said.

When I turned to him, he grabbed my hand in his meaty paw and murmured, "Thanks."

❖❖

113

In the rain, the frame two-storey looked even more of a dump. I sat in the car a few doors away, nursing my last Craven "A", pretending to case the place before storming its barricades. In fact, I was trying to summon up Georgia's kind of courage to go in. There didn't seem to be any activity behind its faded walls. And Georgia's mistreated green Buick was nowhere in sight on the street. I'd probably missed her. Yet I couldn't shake the suspicion that the house held something malevolent. *If you really believe that, Rudnicki, move your fanny.*

I decided on a direct assault. If the front door on the porch wasn't open, I'd scout the rear. I eased up the paint-peeled stairs and peered through the cloudy etched-glass window of the door. Nothing. Turning the handle, I gently pushed the door a smidgen. No creak. Opening it wider, I stepped inside, making sure my dress Timberlands were soundless on the bowed hardwood floors. The hallway smelled. Of damp and mould, of old grease and smoke, and of something sweet yet indefinable.

"Georgia?" My voice crackling with tension, her name emerged in a loud whisper. I called out again. The silence coiled itself around me like the chill of the house.

Then, somewhere on the second storey, I heard a scuttling sound. Now a shattering noise—a crystal chandelier exploding onto a ballroom floor. A thud, a yelp of pain. "Georgia!" I took the steps two at a time to the upstairs. Rushed into a bedroom at the back where the racket had erupted. Nobody. The window behind the bed was only a hole outlined by shards of glass. I leaped on the bed and looked out on a back yard full of castoff junk—a fridge with its door dangling like a broken wing, an easy chair with the stuffing knocked out of it. And the fleeing form of what looked like a large man in a shiny black raincoat and rubber boots. Obviously injured in the long jump to the ground, the intruder was hobbling round the corner of a garage, turning into the back lane. I raced down the stairs and into a kitchen, wrenched open the back door—and tumbled down a tumbledown staircase.

By the time I pulled myself together—three seconds, tops— and reached the alley, there was no sign of the person. Limping, I ran to the cross street and went up and down it, as far as the nearest intersections, looking for any hint of the figure in black. Nothing. That's when I spotted Georgia's Buick, one street over from her house. Clever girl. The car was unlocked but empty. Rummaging quickly around in the glove compartment, I found little more than a leaking pack of McDonald's ketchup on top of a wrinkled map of the city. It had stained the map the colour of blood.

Where the hell was Georgia? I returned to her house the front way. This time I shouted her name. And a couple of times more as I stood in the hall. The calls resounded up the stairwell.

The person who'd leaped through the upstairs window was probably looking for the same prize I was. Right: a thorough search. First, the fireplace. Half a century ago, the livingroom may have bespoken elegance. Traces remained of paisley wallpaper and a plate shelf that once circled the walls. Now the place was dark with decades of grime, the floors sagged, and the few pieces of furniture wouldn't make the cut at a thrift shop.

The façade of the brick fireplace was so black, somebody might have taken a blowtorch to it. The art-deco tiles that formed the hearth were worn and faded. And stained with what looked like fresh soot.

I grabbed an old McDonald's take-out bag lying nearby, knelt on it and began shifting the charcoal remnants of logs that were old enough to be fossilized. I felt for any loose bricks inside the fireplace. Poked blindly around in the flue, which was open. All I came up with were filthy hands. If the diary had been there once, it was gone now.

Maybe it hadn't been hidden in the fireplace after all. Despite the dankness of the house, I was sweating as I threw off rotting cushions and rooted around and under a dun-colored sofa. That exhausted all possible hiding-places in the living-room. A parlor—too grand a name for the room it had become—was awash in cardboard boxes. Though most were empty, a few had their lids closed and looked full. Lifting the cartons one at a time onto an arborite-topped kitchen table, I went through them carefully. The first three contained neatly folded pieces of women's clothing. Skirts, blouses, the odd feminine undergarment that left me unsettled, given the muddled sex of the wearer. The next one had a surprising collection of men's things—designer-label ties, a few Byblos shirts, a pair of Sperry Top-Sider boots, and a gold Rolex with a cracked crystal and frozen hands. Things too good to toss away, even if you were no longer a man.

The final box was jammed with books, hardcovers and paperbacks, all on the same theme. A medical text titled *Transsexualism and Sex Reassignment.* A weathered old volume stolen from the library, *Man Into Woman.* And a much newer one which seemed the most-thumbed, and studded with notes in the margins—*Emergence: A Transsexual Autobiography*, about a woman who'd become a man named Mario. The corner of one page was turned down and exclamation marks framed a paragraph that began:

> The females-to-males I met seemed to fall into a constructive general pattern: Outwardly, they were more or less like anyone else. They set their life goals, completed their sex reassignments, continued their education, married, built homes and families. Most of these females who came for sex-change surgery made little fuss and, when discharged, quietly left the hospital without incident.

Then, for a moment, I thought I'd reached the motherlode. Interesting as these books might have been, what they were

116

hiding seemed even more fascinating. Buried in the bottom of the box was something called *The Nothing Book*. I remembered seeing it in a stationery store: a book of blank white pages. Perfect for a diary. I opened it up in the middle. Blank. Turned to the front. Still virgin white. Riffled through every page with my thumb. Nothing.

And nothing else in the parlor. Nothing in the downstairs bathroom, except for the dregs of cosmetics in the medicine cabinet. Nothing in the kitchen but scraps of food in the cupboards and a recently deceased mouse behind the stove.

Upstairs. The back bedroom, with a gaping wound where the window had been, wouldn't take long. When I got there, its cupboard was bare. I knew how the poor doggie felt. The drawers in an ugly assemble-it-yourself dresser yielded only bobby pins and a torn brassiere. No diary taped conveniently behind its mirror. I looked under the bed and emerged with a noseful of dust balls. I was just about at the point of agreeing with Stephen Leacock: *If at first you don't succeed, quit, quit at once.*

Just about. But more as an act of frustration than anything, I yanked the bed away from the wall. Something solid slapped the floor below the window. I dragged the bed back even further and hurried around to the headboard. There, splayed on the floorboards, lay a wonderful black book with terrific embossed gold letters that spelled out that delicious word: DIARY.

I picked it up carefully with the corner of a filthy sheet that forlornly covered the bed. This was no nothing book. Its pages were crammed with a graceful feminine script, far from Georgia's hurried scribble on the restaurant serviette. The inside front cover confirmed it was hers: "If found, please return to Georgia West. Telephone . . . " —all in the same handwriting as in the rest of the diary. I would read it later, in the comfort of my car, before giving it to Daniela. Loosening my belt a notch, I slipped the plump volume inside my shirt in the back, where it was concealed by my loose-fitting cord jacket. I walked casually to the Mini and put on a pair of work gloves before burying the diary under maps in the glove compartment.

After strolling back to the house, I decided to do a final cursory search of the upstairs. The bedroom across the hall was absolutely barren of anything but a funny smell. A stench that must be coming from a bathroom. Georgia must have left in a helluva hurry.

That could be the door to the john there. I went to open it, but the warped door was jammed. I put my shoulder to it and pushed. It opened enough for me to see the bathtub.

Georgia hadn't left.

The nude body was sprawled in the tub. The head was lolling to one side. The eyes were wide open and vacant. Vivid blue bruises ringed the neck. The rest of the body was bathed in a sticky sea of blood. Blood that had poured from two patches of grievously wounded flesh. Flesh where Georgia's hormone-enhanced, surgically assembled breasts had been.

❖❖

13

A Time
to Speak

❖❖

I'd felt like fainting as I staggered back out of the bathroom. I'd run to the bedroom, climbed on the bed, stuck my head out the window frame and heaved in great gulps of fresh, wet air. Somehow those artistic slayings in the movies and those antiseptic homicide descriptions in the papers can never prepare you for the breath-catching jolt of a real murder.

The old man next door hadn't wanted to answer my battering of fists. When he finally did, I'd pushed my way past his protesting form to the phone in his shadowy hall. A patrol car had responded to my coolly delivered call within minutes. Just enough time for me to rinse the incriminating fireplace soot from my hands. Within half an hour, an already irritated Inspector Phil Rusk had arrived, informed in advance that somebody named Dan Rudnicki had discovered a body.

❖❖

The inspector, his cigar lit before he even stepped into the house, had grilled me tersely and had me retrace my steps. I'd told him how I came to be there. Mentioned going through the boxes—looking for nothing specific, I said. Not a word about the hidden diary, which I wanted to read first. Then Rusk had insisted on taking me back to the bathroom. And its blood bath.

I'd braced myself to look again at the mutilated body. Tried not to see her frozen face, her ballooning eyes. Instead, I'd seen ragged chunks of flesh at the far end of the tub, smeared with congealing blood. Her breasts. Investigating officers in latex gloves were soundlessly checking the room and taking photographs, their expressions as blank as Georgia's.

Now Phil Rusk was seated across from me at the arborite table, pursuing the notion that I was probably responsible for her death. He knew I wasn't, in his heart of hearts, but he was exacting his revenge because of my pain-in-the-butt presence here. And, I figured, because of his general annoyance that the case against Burt Gold was falling apart in front of him.

"I guess if Gold is still in Riverview—as he was when I visited him there yesterday—he couldn't have done this one," I said provocatively. "And based on what the doctors told me, he didn't seem capable of doing the first one."

"You were allowed in to see Gold? He's in protective custody," Rusk said.

"Maybe they were impressed by my bedside manner."

"I'll be following this up, Rudnicki, and if you used any deception to see Burt Gold, you will be stripped of your licence. In any event, you are in much more serious trouble at the moment. I am not overly swayed by the fact that it was you who made the call about the body. Further, this homicide does not preclude the very real likelihood that Gold committed the earlier one. As even you should be aware, this could well be a copycat murder."

"Look, Inspector, with all due respect, you're wasting time. I'm convinced it was Breen who killed Georgia. As I've already told you. She was running scared from him. You can check that out with her friend Martini. As I've explained. You should be going after Breen. He probably killed Bobbi Flynn too. That's based on my own brush with him—which you say your people filed a report on, even though I didn't press charges. The man's a rabid, marauding animal. Compared to him, Gold's a tame little housepet. Anyway, in one of his more lucid moments, Burt Gold told me he was drinking with Barney O'Malley when he was supposed to be killing Flynn."

"We checked that out with O'Malley, who was in fact nowhere near Gold at the time."

"Where was he?"

Rusk sighed. It was always a bad sign. "I'm conducting this investigation, Rudnicki. Your uninformed fumblings are fouling the nest. To be ignorant of one's ignorance is the malady of the ignorant."

A quotation: that was even worse. And the worst thing was I didn't have a snappy quote as a comeback.

"A constable will take you down to the station," he said, standing up to dismiss me, "and eventually I will be there to take a statement about your infuriating involvement in this business."

As I said at the start of all this, the waiting is always the worst. In this case, waiting for an irate homicide inspector to take a statement when he wants to make you suffer. He left me dangling for three hours in the Public Safety Building before having a stenographer place my words on the record. During the wait, I had too much time to consider what would have happened if I'd skipped that cigarette outside Georgia's house.

Would I have walked into the murder well under way? Or—crueller thought—could I have prevented it if I'd arrived sooner? Rusk was no help. Every time I veered into speculation or tried to extract any information about either killing, he cut me off with the graciousness of a guillotine. It was nearly six in the afternoon before I was allowed to leave, uncharged, and since breakfast I hadn't eaten anything but crow.

From a grimy pay phone down the block, I called the studio and then the phone number I had for Graves, to tell my client I had found Georgia, once and for all. No answer at either. I took a cab to my car, trying not to look at the darkened death house, and drove home to my own dank but life-filled place. Shevchenko welcomed me with a glare, then fell back to sleep. Within minutes, I'd opened a can of Beans with Pork and bolted it cold. Good thing the girls weren't around to see this dietary sacrilege. Delivered from immediate starvation, I more measuredly scrambled some eggs with peppers and onions into a mess of *huevos rancheros*. They went down almost as fast because I couldn't wait to learn if Georgia's diary held any answers to either murder.

I'd carried the book in with the work gloves, which I now donned again. With a fire lit, I stretched out on the cushiony living-room sofa and began to read. Her elegant, large-looped handwriting had filled nearly all the lined pages of the thick black diary. It was one of those timeless ones with days of the week in place of printed dates. Georgia had dated the entries herself, with the first more than three years earlier, on a New Year's Day.

I will be a woman, it began. *I will do all that I must to transform this cursed body and become as wholly female in form as I feel in mind and spirit. This diary will be an account of my journey, which really began more than twenty years ago. Ever since I was a child—was it at three? four?—have been praying to whatever God there was in my life to magically transmute me into my true sex. At first Mom and even Dad found it amusing as I dressed up in her clothes and tripped around in her old high-heeled shoes. They laughed when they saw me with a couch pillow under her old housecoat to make me appear pregnant. Their laughing turned to puzzlement when I started school and they realized I wasn't interested in playing with the other boys in kindergarten. And one of the few times I can recall Dad spanking me was when I was six and he caught me touching the tiny perfect vulva of Sonya, my best friend. He didn't understand that it wasn't sexual in the way he imagined; I merely wanted to see what I was missing, what I wanted in myself.*

Why was it a little boy couldn't play with dolls, but a little girl could be a tomboy —in jeans and short hair —and play war and baseball with the boys? I've talked to a man who made the transition from female to male and he says his childhood fantasies of being a boy were nowhere near as traumatic as mine. As a girl-child, she could deny her birth-sex under masculine clothes and even announce openly that she wanted to be a boy, without her parents insisting on taking her to a shrink —as mine eventually did.

The diary continued over the next few days with more memories from Georgia's growing-up years. Slights, humiliations, hidden anger—which welled over when she left home for Vancouver to attend university and realized the academic community was no more forgiving of sexual confusion than a little sawmill town in the Interior. Fearful of the possibility that she was simply a homosexual, she found it agonizing to room with other boys in residence. The few times she hesitantly chanced conventional dates, she found herself turning the conversation to what the girls wore and how they did their hair. Sometimes she was sexually aroused in their company. But confused about wanting to *be* them even as she wanted to *have* them, the sex was never consummated. There was no comfort in her studies, either. She learned of the Greek prophet Tiresias whose male-to-female transsexual state had been a punishment from the gods. And when Tiresias began to revel in her new identity, they'd turned her back into a man.

After Georgia got her English lit degree, padded with

❖❖

several courses in psychology, she took what sounded like a menial job at an ad agency. Early on, the diary summed up her several years of visits to a string of psychiatrists in Vancouver, none of them any consolation. Then after about a month's entries, it mentioned that she had just seen a new shrink who promised to refer her to a gender identity specialist. Because Canadian doctors were no longer performing transsexual operations, she'd have to go to one of the few places where they were still being done under responsible supervision—a clinic in Colorado. *Finally, the world will know me as I am.*

It wouldn't take the world long. Georgia had detailed the extraordinary journey she'd undertaken over the next couple of years. Two hours' worth of reading, so absorbing I forgot to light up a cigarette or relight the fire. In Colorado, she had to run the gauntlet of two psychiatrists, a social worker and an endocrinologist. They soon told her she'd have to live and work day and night as a mock woman for at least a year before the first operation. Actually being encouraged to cross-dress in public was a welcome relief. So was all the estrogen they shot into her backside to gentle her along into her new gender. Within days, she was feeling an itchiness in her male breasts; within a couple of weeks, they were protruding like a twelve-year-old's. Soon she was waking up in the middle of the night, surprised by the pain in her breasts when she rolled on to her stomach too fast. Later, her neck, arms and wrists shrank in size. Soft feminine fat replaced hard male muscle. She let her dark locks lengthen as her facial hair retreated. Even though Georgia had become sexually impotent, she felt more alive than she ever had. She joyfully donated all but the most expensive of her male clothing and jewellery to the Sally Ann.

The excitement at her transformation seemed to blinker her from the scary reality of the rest of her life. Her treatments and travel costs were being covered by the B.C. government medical plan. But her job in the agency had ended with her coming out. Her relationship with her confused and guilt-

124

wracked parents was in tatters. She was now living on welfare. Then the government announced that—with many in the Canadian medical establishment no longer considering sex changes respectable—it was cancelling its coverage of transsexual operations.

Oh lord, I'm going to be a goddam modern-day Tiresias, Georgia wrote. *Man becoming woman—and now back to loathsome man again. I have no money, no hope of getting and holding a job in my limbo condition, no hope of . . . hope.*

She had her evolving body, however, one that she found could be disguised effectively enough to fool some men. If transvestites could get away with it just by playing dress-up, why not her—whose body was already halfway to womanhood? The diary diligently chronicled her first forays into picking men up in a bar and her fumbled attempts at satisfying their loathesome bodies without penetration. The drunker they were, the easier it was. She was astonished at the amount of money she could earn.

Enough to buy her the first major operation in Colorado. Castration. *I woke up crying yesterday morning and, although I have never felt so much pain, I was weeping tears of peace and rapture. They've removed my testicles and turned my penis inside out like the finger of a glove. They used the skin to create my labia, my very own vulva. They made me look like Sonya!*

Now Georgia needed more money to finish the job, to have her very own vagina. Back she came to Vancouver, where she was more comfortable practising as a prostitute and where she had a friend in the same fix, Daniela Martini. And where, one night, she met an initially charming Donny Breen. (The diary conveniently recorded his phone number, a fact I filed away.) Because I knew its climax, the story of their meeting had a horrible poignancy. From the start, she knew he was a pimp, though not a crack dealer. But he was so solicitous and so full of promises of the good life they would share. Georgia allowed herself to lean on a man—to trust one—for the only time in her life. That account of their first night was the diary's single mention of him by name. Everywhere else, Breen became simply "he" or "him," as if he were the only male that mattered in her cruel, contained world.

The honeymoon lasted two weeks. One slow night, crazed on coke, unable to get her to snort any, he beat her senseless. So she was too frightened to deny him, not long after, when he told her she was taking on an interesting trick, somebody a little kinky, somebody who worked in the movies.

It was only then that I noticed the next few pages of the diary had been raggedly knifed out. Damn.

But maybe I wasn't missing anything vital. The following page opened almost at the beginning of her first session in Bobbi Flynn's hotel room. Georgia felt sickened and strangely ashamed. Yet there were promises of more money than Breen ever expected from any trick. Money she could hide from him for her operation. She let herself be dragged into several evenings of perverse sex, gorged with trussings and grotesque acts that the diary only hinted at. Bobbi, who'd known about Georgia's condition from Breen, became fascinated with it— *toying with me like a little girl with a new Barbie,* Georgia wrote. *"You're partway in purgatory, halfway to heaven," Bobbi said. Then she puts me through a hell of degradation and self-disgust.*

At first, out of some protective instinct, the overawed Georgia hadn't even dared to write down the movie star's full name —just her initials. Later, she came back and carefully replaced each "B.F." with "Bobbi Flynn" or "Bobbi" in her distinctive script. Apparently, after the sordidness of their encounters, she was no longer inclined to veil the identity of her famous trick.

There was a more cryptic reference in the diary a few days later. *Last night, as a way of taunting Bobbi, I told her I wasn't the only transsexual she knew —there was someone else involved in her life now who was making the journey. I wouldn't tell her who B. was. She wheedled and coaxed me. Finally, I felt I had some power over her. She promised me beautiful presents if I told —what did I want? I said she'd be surprised at B.'s true gender. She tried to scoff at me, saying it couldn't be anyone on the picture, she knew every important person on the set, and who else did we know in common? She said I was just lying to get at her. Then I'm lying, I said. But I'm not. What sex is B.? — at least tell me that, she insisted. She's a he, but he isn't really, I said. She slapped me then, hard. When she saw that violence wouldn't get her anywhere—I'd been beaten up by a master, I told her—that's when she offered me double and eventually triple the money she'd ever paid me before. Yes, I did tell her. She pretended not to be too surprised, and not very interested in who B. turned out to be. "Him? He's not important in my life."*

Oh god, I wish I hadn't told. I had promised B. the secret would be safe with me. Damn my desperation! Desperation that would make me betray someone who's experiencing the same agonies I am —no matter how unlikable a human being B. is.

The scattered entries that followed were a patchwork document of Georgia's life through the next couple of weeks. These went up to the end of March, only about a month before I was reading the diary. There was no mention of Bobbi Flynn or the enigmatic B. They related her dealings with other tricks. Her increasing compulsion to escape the violence of Donny Breen. And the loving support she was getting from her only friend, Daniela—*who knows most things about me.*

Bloody hell. It looked like another group of pages, maybe eight or ten of them, had been cut out of the diary. Then it continued. One brief passage, undated, written in a more hurried hand—almost a scrawl—yet recognizably hers:

I can't stand it anymore. Keeping quiet made sense when I didn't suspect who had killed Bobbi. I had some crazy loyalty, but that means nothing now. How could I have let that blind me to the horror of what was happening all around me—a horror I had some unconscious hand in. Last night, a detective who was working for Bobbi's parents forced me to talk to him (but he gave me money) and I almost told him everything. But I couldn't—I was so terrified. Now, I must.

One of the only things I remember from my church-going days as a child is a passage from Ecclesiastes, those wonderful lines about all things having their season. There's a part that goes, if I can remember it . . .

A time to rend, and a time to sew,

A time to keep silence, and a time to speak . . .

This is my time to speak.

I unfolded from the sofa, stretched the kinks out of my still-sore body, and halfheartedly stirred the embers in the fireplace. What had the horrified Georgia been about to tell? That Breen had killed Bobbi Flynn? And who was B.? *She's a he, but he isn't really.* Was it the same person who'd removed all the offending passages (and why didn't she/he take the whole diary)? Most frustrating of all, one of the missing sections would have covered the crucial period leading up to the night of the murder, and its aftermath.

Only one person might know who B. is: Daniela, who knew most things about Georgia. Oh, hell, but did she even know her friend had been murdered? In my mindless impatience to read the diary, I hadn't even taken the trouble to tell Daniela. I had her number from the *Criss-Cross* directory. After her phone rang several times, I was about to hang up when a rough facsimile of Daniela's deep voice said, "Yeah?"

"It's Dan Rudnicki. Have you heard?"

His sudden wail, like a wounded whelp's cry for its mother, gave me my answer. It continued for a minute or more before I broke in. "Daniela, I'm sorry. I'm sorry it happened, I'm sorry I was too late to stop it from happening."

"I—I heard. The police were over here . . . They just left a half-hour ago."

"Did you tell them about the diary?"

"Yeah, I told them everythin'. About you comin' here, and goin' after Georgia. And all about that animal Breen. How could he do that to anyone so beautiful and gentle as Georgia!"

"How could anyone do that to anyone. Look, I have the diary, and I've read it."

"The diary." His mind was re-grouping. "Does it say anythin' about Breen? Is there anythin' in there that'll nail him for what he did to her?"

"It'll help. But there are some pages torn out in a couple of places. And she wrote about somebody she identified only with the initial B. Another transsexual. Do you have any idea who that is? It might have been one of her tricks, or maybe a friend, or just somebody she'd met casually. She said it would surprise people if they knew this person's real sex."

He thought. Eventually, he said, "No. No, just a few days ago, when she first came here, she told me she was goin' to sit down with me when things settled down. Tell me all the stuff that'd been happenin' to her. I knew about Bobbi Flynn, but she said she had some big surprises— secrets she wouldn't tell anyone else. But she was always on the run, too tired to talk when she came back here to sleep...Couldn't B. stand for Bobbi Flynn?"

"No, she mentions this person to Bobbi."

"Then maybe . . . no, that would be too fuckin' weird."

"What would?"

"That it would mean Breen."

I'd wondered the same thing. "Maybe it's not so weird. He likes to hang around transsexuals—maybe he's really one in the making."

"I think I could tell."

"Takes one to know one? You're probably right . . . Listen, Daniela, Georgia said some very loving things about you in her diary. I'll make a copy of those pages for you before I figure out how to hand it over to the police tomorrow. Anonymously."

"You might not have a hope in hell, Dan. I told them about the diary maybe bein' over at Georgia's old place, and the cop said maybe you had it, and they were sure goin' to find out, fast. And I wasn't s'posed to talk to you about it."

❖❖

After a few more fruitless words of consolation, I hung up, fast, and started dialing 911—the quickest way I knew to get through to Rusk. He wasn't in, a desk sergeant named Grimmer told me after I'd been switched to his line. Could he help?

Yep, sure could, I said. Good old Dan Rudnicki had found a piece of evidence that might have some bearing on the Georgia West murder and, as a responsible citizen, he'd like to make sure it got into the proper hands right away.

Which is when an insistent ringing reverberated through the house. Someone leaning long and hard on the door chimes. Someone who could only be a wrathful Phil Rusk.

14

Terminated

❖❖

I'd told Grimmer to hold while I got the door. It was Rusk, all right, belching smoke, some of it from his cigar. His face looked drawn and even more pinched than usual. "Inspector, you're out late. Come in." He had another plainclothes with him, a beefy but subservient fellow who followed his boss into the hallway.

"I intend to ask you only two questions, Rudnicki," the Inspector said, pulling on the cigar and exhaling a putrid cloud, "and how you answer them may decide your professional future, if I can dignify it with that phrase."

"Shoot. Of course, that's just a euphemism, Inspector."

"One: Did you know that Georgia West was keeping a diary?"

"Of course. Didn't everyone?"

He refused to let the sarcasm incense him any further. "And two: Do you now have said diary in your possession?"

"Of course. As I was just telling—"

"Not another word." The well-spaced syllables were delivered in a deliberate, don't-fool-with-me voice. "Produce the diary, this second, and then get your coat. Withholding evidence—*concealing* evidence—spells the conclusion of your career, such as it was."

This was all beginning to sound like Archie Goodwin Meets Inspector Cramer. "Am I allowed to hang up the phone?" I said, beckoning to the livingroom. "It wouldn't be fair to keep Sergeant Grimmer dangling forever."

Rusk's face went into eclipse. "Was Grimmer trying to reach me here?"

"That's *three* questions. No, I was trying to reach you there."

The inspector seemed loath to phrase a fourth question. ". . . Why?"

"Because, as you can confirm with the sergeant himself, I was attempting to let you know that somehow the diary got into my car that was parked near Georgia West's place."

"*Somehow. I know* how."

"No, you don't. It could have been dumped there by the guy I saw fleeing the scene. And I retrieved the diary when I got home, and after looking through it—"

"You handled it?"

"Only with those work gloves on the table over there. And after *carefully* looking through it to determine what it was, I tried to contact you and got Grimmer instead."

Rusk glanced at his slender, expensive Seiko. "You spent an outrageously long time looking before you called."

"I didn't tell you when I retrieved it. And, I admit, it was fascinating reading."

Rusk waved a hand to dismiss my prattling. "Where's the phone?"

He spoke quickly, quietly into the receiver and listened for a few seconds before hanging up.

Silently, I handed him the diary, which I'd just packed in a plastic bag from the kitchen. Without a word, he took it and passed it off to the big cop beside him. Rusk wheeled and headed for the door.

The two of them, still mute, were letting themselves out when I said, "You might be interested in a page—oh, about a quarter of the way through the thing—that has a phone number. Somebody you might want to talk to. A guy by the name of Donny Breen."

I should have felt some sort of smug relief at escaping Rusk's clutches again. But my sleep that night was shot through with images of baby seals being clubbed and butchered. I woke up wanting to talk to Larissa and Esther. When I called the music camp, I got a woman who identified herself as the cook. She was in the middle of a stew, no one else was around, and the girls were rehearsing. Oh, all right, she'd stop what she was doing and try to find them. Never mind, she knew *exactly* what Larissa Rudnicki looked like.

Several minutes later, someone spoke. At first I couldn't decipher the whisper of a voice. Finally, it said, so softly it might have beamed from the moon, "Hello, Dad."

"Is that you, Larissa? What's the matter?" There was a mutter. "I can't hear you. Speak louder. Are you okay?"

"Oh, I'm...fine. I guess." Then, slightly stronger, "Yeah, I'm fine. Don't worry."

"Larissa, is your sister there?"

After much juggling, and the phone crashing to the floor, Esther came on the line. She sounded more enthusiastic until I asked, "What's the matter with Larissa?"

Dead air. Obviously a hand covering the mouthpiece and some murmuring in the background. Esther returned. "I can't tell you. She made me promise."

"Can't tell me what? S.T., I want to know what's the matter with your sister. Now."

"She said if I told she'd take all my Archie comics and flush them down the toilet."

"Esther, put . . . Larissa . . . back . . . on the line."

"Mr. Rudnicki?" It was the cook. "The camp nurse is here. She wants to talk to you."

Oh God.

"This is Miss Dunbar. Is that Larissa's father?" A pause. "Larissa," I heard in muffled tones, "you and Esther can go back to the practice now. No, I have to talk to him. No, I know what you said. I'll talk to you during break . . . Mr. Rudnicki? Now, please don't worry. Physically, your daughter is well. But she's very upset."

"Would you please tell me what's going on?"

"Certainly." She had a crisp British accent. "I understand there is no Mrs. Rudnicki. That would help explain this. Larissa has been finding it quite difficult to contemplate discussing this with you."

"This—what?"

"You must also realize that your daughter is quite protective of you."

"Miss Dunbar, if you don't tell me what's wrong with my daughter in the next ten seconds, I will charter a helicopter and fly over to Bowen and land it in your lap."

"There is absolutely no need to be aggressive, Mr. Rudnicki. I was about to tell you that Larissa has experienced the menarche."

"The what?"

"She has menstruated. Had her first . . . period."

Ahhh. "Thank you, Miss Dunbar. Thank you, I appreciate your candour. And your concern. And you can be assured that I will handle this as sensitively as any mother would. Thank you. Please give Larissa my love."

Nadia was at work. "Dan! We've got to talk!"

"And how are you, Dan? Fine, thank you, Nadia."

"Of course: how *are* you, you poor little boychuk? I heard all the grisly details from Henry on the police beat." She had the journalist's studied skill of distancing herself from disaster by seeing it in terms of a story.

She wanted nonchalance? "I'm well enough, given death, dismemberment and a close encounter of an unkind kind with Phil Rusk. Not to mention having just experienced a momentous rite of passage with my daughter. You must be losing your killer instinct. I expected a call from you yesterday."

"I did try for a couple of hours in the late afternoon—*of course*—but I was tied up all day. On the Bobbi Flynn story, you might be interested to know."

"With who—" The call alert clicked to signal another caller on my line. "Let me get this, Nadge. Be right back." I pumped the phone button and hello'd. It was Adam Graves' secretary, whose name I still knew not. "Mr. Rudnicki? Mr. Graves must see you. Immediately. At the studio." Mentally clicking my heels, I agreed to be seen, immediately. "That was Graves, Nadia. Wants me there right away. Why don't we get together later?"

"This afternoon? About one? My place? If you can't make it, call me at work. Oh, and you might not know: Henry says Rusk has decided not to charge Burt Gold after all. As soon as Riverview says he's okay, he's free to leave."

My trips up to Cypress Studios were becoming more and more foreboding. I knew how the sun felt that morning, attempting an end run around a front line of bruised-looking clouds. The universe seemed out of sorts, as miserable as I was. k.d. had no song sorrowful enough to express my mood.

The hubbub I usually heard around the studio was missing. The only crew I spotted outside went about their business quietly. The few people inside nodded, if anything. Graves' secretary was less warm, if possible. Her eyes—what I could see of them shuttered behind bright-red forelocks—told me that I meant trouble. She tonelessly acknowledged me and let Graves know via intercom of my arrival. Without even a pretence at polite conversation, we waited for the Great Man to summon me into his presence. And waited. I was starting to feel distinctly out of favour by the time he buzzed her to send me in.

Seeing the two of them there caught me off guard. Barney O'Malley, a full tumbler of golden liquid in hand, was lolling on a leather couch across from the liquor cabinet where Graves was pouring himself a cognac.

"Rinicky."

"Gentlemen."

Back now behind the barricade of his man-sized desk, Graves looked as chippy as a Churchill with the cigar plucked from his lips. He was wearing more beard than I'd ever seen on him. That, and what seemed a lack of sleep, made his full face even puffier. The cognac he was quaffing wasn't helping a helluva lot.

"You've heard?" I asked, sitting in the chair with casters, cautiously.

"Everything, kiddo. But not from you. Who I've been paying."

"If you know everything, you know I was otherwise occupied yesterday until late in the evening—when I called you here and at home."

"So tell him what he doesn't know." O'Malley spoke for the first time, listing to the starboard side of the couch as he shifted his girth.

I told, giving him all the detail I figured a conscientious investigator should provide a paying client. The last four frenetic days. Starting with my stakeout and pursuit of Georgia. The fifty bucks' worth of information she gave me about her big bruiser of a pimp. Then—before I could convince Georgia to see Graves again—Donny Breen's sudden arrival and our altercation in the alley.

Here, my client wanted more details. He leaned back in his enormous chair, listening hard. "You managed to fight back and get away from him?"

Should I tell him about my visit to Burt Gold at Riverview? Gold had insisted that he was with O'Malley at the time of Bobbi Flynn's murder. Whereas O'Malley said—and Phil Rusk seemed to believe—Gold wasn't. What the hell.

"...So when I couldn't find Georgia the next day, I decided to spend the time productively and went to see Burt Gold."

O'Malley bobbed up like the prow of a sinking destroyer. "Who told you to see him? Adam, you give him permission to talk to Gold?" He wobbled over to the desk, a daunting figure in all his fat. His body reeked with the stench of Scotch.

Graves' head was shaking determinedly. "No, no. This guy's a disaster." To me: "What a lousy idea. What did you expect to get from a loony anyway?"

"I figured if I couldn't find Georgia West, I might be able to find out who really killed Bobbi Flynn. Which would be just as good as locating your alibi. A couple of people on the picture, people I've come to respect, weren't convinced he did it."

"Which people?" O'Malley wanted to know.

"Leo Garrett and Jennie Barlow. You yourself told me, right here in this office, that most people didn't think he could murder anything but a screenplay. And while it might have been a long shot, I felt if Burt wasn't too far gone, he might be able to illuminate some of the facts in the case."

"He couldn't ee-loo-min-ate a night light," O'Malley said.

Here goes. "Well, he did have one intriguing thing to say. He said that when Bobbi was killed, you and he were drinking together."

"Christ, that old garbage. I already admitted to the cops I

had a couple of drinks with Gold. *Early* that night. Went back to my room at the Pan Pacific. Ordered up room service—just about the time it was all happening. And the cops say the hotel has a timed record of bringing me the corned beef and cabbage." His blue polka-dot bowtie kept vaulting in synch with his vocalizing. "What else you want?"

"Nothing. I'm simply reporting what Burt Gold told me. So perhaps I didn't get much useful from him. Do you want to hear how I found Georgia West—finally?" They did. I told them about her friend, Martini, and their fear of Breen. How I went to her house to find her. Pressed by Graves, I gave more detail than I'd intended about the murder scene. He appeared genuinely shaken.

As he did a few minutes later, when I mentioned Georgia's diary. Purposely focussed on him, I was watching for the reaction I got. Sheer surprise.

"Diary? You found a diary?"

"Don't panic. You're not in it. I had a chance to read through the whole thing before I turned it over to the police."

"Who else did that hooker have in there?" O'Malley asked.

"Besides Bobbi and Breen? Nobody you'd know. A couple of sections are missing, one of them around the time of the first murder. There's another frustrating thing: Georgia mentions someone she calls only by an initial: B. A fellow transsexual. Any idea who that might be?"

Graves was gazing down at his drained cognac glass. "Are you asking me?" he said, looking up.

"Hey, how the hell would Adam know some whore's friends?" O'Malley said.

"How about you, O'Malley?"

"Never had the pleasure of meeting West," he said, shuffling back to the couch. "Anyway, sounds like it's her friend Breen she's describing. Didn't think he was a transsexual, though. Looks like he's the bad guy in both these cases."

"The police seem to think so. They've decided not to press charges against Burt Gold."

This time they weren't surprised, having already heard from the police, who'd asked Graves if he now wanted to charge Gold with attempted manslaughter. He didn't, when they told him Gold would be staying safely in hospital for the foreseeable future. O'Malley lurched to his feet, in what I soon realized was his symbolic attempt to end the discussion. "So," he told me, "I guess Adam won't be needing your services anymore."

Graves was as taken aback as I was. "Barney, I've been thinking. With Breen still out there... and the kid here already coming out okay from one run-in with him . . . Maybe I could use a bodyguard."

"You want a bodyguard, get a real one up from the States. Not some half-pint who doesn't even pack a gun. Nothing personal, Danny boy. Those are just the facts."

Barney O'Malley, the publicity man, was clearly in charge of this session. Saying nothing, Adam Graves, the executive producer, turned his palms up in a gesture of surrender.

"I'll send you my bill," I told Graves, ignoring his puppeteer.

"Sure. Add a couple of extra days to the tab for all your trouble. We'll pay upon receipt, kiddo," he said, trying to mollify me.

Walking through the outer office without even a nod to his secretary, I stepped outside as Bob Melts drove up in an apple-red Ferrari. The director followed his beard out of the car, looked askance at me, and said, "Aren't you that detective chap?"

I went over to offer my name and my hand, which he took tentatively. "Any news on this damnable upset? It's all over the telly: two murders now, the same ghastly *modus operandi,* and they're still casting Burt Gold as a killer."

After I disabused him of that notion, he asked me what

Graves was having me do these days. Explaining my recent unemployment, I thought his reaction shot—a look of pain—was a little overplayed. But I was prepared to take any show of compassion at face value. Melts wanted to know how intimately I'd been involved in the events of the past few days. As he listened to the skeletal details, his brow lifted and his head kept bobbing up and down in what could pass as sympathy.

"I must know simply *everything*," he soon interrupted. "I don't care if Adam Graves believes your usefulness has ended. It's vital I hear about the relationship between poor Bobbi and that transsexual person. You've had the opportunity to peruse most of the diary? And it incriminates no one by name? Let us *please* arrange a meeting posthaste."

He was about to tie himself up in a financial meeting with Graves. Most of the cast and crew were out on location, where he'd left them with the second-unit director. But the next day he was driving up to a new location for a fresh look at the setting and a re-think of camera angles. We could talk on the way up and back. I agreed to join him.

Of all the areas of the city to be gentrified, none is more unlikely than the Downtown East Side. Just east of Chinatown, where the drifters flock, the rubbies and junkies. Loggers with limbs yanked off by yarding machines, sailors with minds snapped by the lethal mix of the sea and the sauce. Welfare families have to rent doddering wooden two-storeys weather-stained to a tarnished silver. Now they're experiencing the added sting of living beside two-income couples who own new Victorian-styled sub-divides tarted up in trendy blues and yellows. Or living next door to a high-income single woman like Nadia who'd lavished forty-five thousand on an old house just to gut and gussy it up.

Nadia argued that people like her were supporting the local

economy, the Portuguese butchers and the Japanese grocers, and generally enriching the district. She thrived on its yeastiness and sighed at my worries over her safety here. Actually, the only person in any trouble at the moment was me. Rounding the rim of the public park across from her place, I was jogging at a slug's stroll while Nadia romped ahead of me. The sun had deigned to appear this afternoon. On the field, school kids of several colourations had slipped the confines of their phys ed class to play baseball on the grass. Around a sandbox, Chinese grandmothers tended impossibly small babies in white bonnets. Two Indian men of indeterminate age sat on a park bench and inhaled the ancient ocean scents that still escaped from the downtown harbour.

All this I was noticing between grunts and gasps and a final plea for Nadia to relent. She did another quarter lap before crossing the field and plunking down on the damp lawn where I'd collapsed. "I'm still panting more than you are," I pointed out. "You should take up smoking."

"I'd rather wreck my heart with a hit of coffee. Come on," she said, standing up without a push from her arms. I struggled to my feet the way the rest of the world does and sidled with her to the white gingerbread cottage across the street. The interior was as shiny and streamlined as the inside of an oyster shell. No little doodads, no doilies, no dust.

Resuscitating the espresso machine in her perfect little kitchen, Nadia returned to the subject we'd started on before her daily demon run: Larissa's first period. "If you don't think you can handle talking about it, Dan," she said, "don't louse things up by trying. Let me sit down with her. We already spoke about it the night of the Bryan Adams concert. She was ready for it, welcoming it even."

"Really?"

"Oh sure, she saw it as a big step in growing up, being a woman. She just didn't think you'd be comfortable talking about it."

"Listen, Nadge, given everything that's been happening, all the sad people I've seen who are devastated about being captives in the wrong sex, I'm ecstatic about Larissa's attitude towards being a woman. If she doesn't want to discuss it with me yet—"

"Or maybe ever—"

"Or ever—that's fine. As long as she can talk to you. Although I wish she could bring herself to share it with me somehow."

We decided I should be patient, open, loving—nothing but what you'd expect of any perfect parent.

That settled, we discussed another drama in real life: My discovery of Georgia's body. Like a good reporter, Nadia asked only those questions that propelled the story along. For the first time, I felt I had a truly compassionate audience. And by the time I finished describing the contents of the diary, she was near tears. She kept pressing me about what they revealed of Georgia's personality, and the transsexual's psyche.

"Look, this is one of the few times I agree with my brother-in-law. I'm personally appalled at their need to mutilate themselves. I'm not even comfortable with the fact that *you* have pierced ears. But I've also witnessed the mental pain that someone like Georgia has endured in a body she really abhorred."

Nadia served our espresso, put out a plate of cookies (ha! store-bought!), and led me into her *Metropolitan Home* living-room. "Yet what bothers me, Dan, is that as a female, she seemed to have become a kind of Real Woman cliché. It's a step backwards to some prefeminist past where women were supposed to be weak, dependent beings."

"I think the saddest thing is that, no matter how many operations she might have had, she would've still been a manufactured female."

"Who could never capitalize on the real power of female biology."

142

"You mean she couldn't have kids . . . . Enough psychology, Nadge. Enough death. I need your help. First, let me tell you about my termination of employment." I enlarged on the scene with dialogue and other dramatic effects.

She asked for more details about the whole morning, including my meeting with Bob Melts. But she homed in on the tag-team of Graves and O'Malley and their reactions to my reports of the diary's contents.

An hour of analyzing what I'd learned and we both agreed we were hunting too hard for mysteries. The most obvious suspect in the murders was Donny Breen. Yet I kept wondering aloud about the other characters who could meet the criteria of the question-mark B. Of them all, O'Malley—Barney—kept surfacing as the one most likely to exceed the bounds of civilized behaviour. First of all, which of us knew what a female-to-male transsexual was supposed to look like? What we did know about Barney was that he was a drunk. Despite that, he had a strange hold on his boss. Was Graves frightened of him because he knew what O'Malley was capable of doing? As I went over the morning's conversation with the two of them, something else niggled at me.

Nadia began to tell me she'd had a chance to talk to O'Malley a couple of days earlier, and—

"*That* was it," I interrupted. "When O'Malley said he'd never met West, he added that he didn't think Breen was a transsexual. How the hell would he think that?"

"Well, Adam Graves knew Georgia. Maybe she described Breen to him and Graves told O'Malley."

Possible, possible. Who else was there? *Bob* Melts—who raised Nadia's suspicions because he was known to have coveted Bobbi Flynn and been jealous of her other liaisons. He also seemed very insistent with me this morning about hearing everything that had happened between Bobbi and Georgia. Yet Melts had such a public career from such an early age, he'd have to have been a very precocious transsexual.

I had another possibility for B., one I wasn't about to mention to Nadia: Jennie Barlow. Maybe it was just my precious male ego, but why had Jennie resisted my advances that day we came back to her place? "I can't," she'd said. And: "It can't go anywhere." She could be a transsexual in transition. I would have known. Sure, just the way the *Province* photographer and everybody else had known about Georgia West.

"And then there's Graves, whom nobody admires. Man, do I wish he was the guilty one."

"You'd have a terrifically hard time convicting him of killing Georgia," Nadia said. "Remember I said I'd talked to Barney O'Malley? And that I was busy all yesterday working on the Bobbi Flynn story? Well, I spent about eight hours supposedly doing a day in the life of a Hollywood producer. Who else but Mr. Adam Graves."

❖❖

15

The
Makher

❖❖

The Austin Mini has been maddening motorists for more than thirty years. Mostly it's bought by women. Maybe they think of it like an A.A. Milne character, cute and lovable and only occasionally cranky. In the old days, I know, less whimsical drivers of both sexes saw it as a practical people carrier that you could run for a penny a mile. Then, in my eyes anyway, it attained a brief burst of respectability when Michael Caine bounced one manfully down a steep flight of stairs in *The Italian Job*. Now it's been overtaken—which isn't too hard—by a whole fleet of bigger, faster, less frustrating small cars. I bought mine only because it was as cheap as borsch. And on sodden days like this, as I sat squashed in the driver's seat, I pondered why I hadn't junked this slow, squat orange crate on wheels. I hoped Bob Melts, in a moment of madness, wouldn't forgo his Ferrari and insist on taking the Mini.

He was late. We'd arranged to meet in the studio parking lot half an hour ago. Which had given me the opportunity to drop off my Invoice for Investigative Services with Graves' grumpy secretary. That still left me time to cuss out the Mini as well as consider the rest of my rendezvous with Nadia the day before.

About the only romantic thing to have happened was our goodbye kiss on the lips. Her eyes had been closed. I peeked. That, and dinner, were all she'd offered. She had speculated, however, on what I'd do now that I was without a client and officially unemployed. Well, I've always believed work is the curse of the working classes. Nadia had a better idea, which she would get back to me on.

She'd already explained her game plan for following up on the Flynn murder—and now, Georgia's. Working through Barney O'Malley, she had pitched Graves on a column about a producer's typical workday, with special emphasis on the business side. It was common knowledge that the film company was looking for additional funding to complete *The Empty Gun*. There was some talk about going public on the Vancouver Stock Exchange to raise capital. A little positive publicity would help, wouldn't it, given all the bad vibes around the picture?

What she'd discovered about Graves personally was little more than I'd learned from the library press clippings. He wouldn't speak in anything but platitudes about Bobbi. Couldn't see any reason why they should be discussing Georgia West. Wisely, he'd wanted to focus the interview on the financial possibilities of film investment. To avoid suspicion, she'd played along. But when asked for a rundown of who did what in the administration office, Graves had been circumspect about O'Malley. He'd preferred to talk generally about the role of the modern ad/pub man, a movie's advertising and publicity person.

Just as I was thinking about him, the devil in question drove by in a white Cutlass rental. Seeing me, Barney O'Malley did a double take, swinging his head around on its fat neck. He jammed the brakes, clambered out of the car and advanced on me, keening. "What are you doing here, Rudnicki? This is private property. You're off the payroll, pal."

At which point a guardian angel, Bob Melts, cruised up in his juicy Italian job, with its straked side panels and the beautiful bellow of what he told me later was a 390bhp flat-12 engine (whatever that is). Lowering his window, he leaned out to hear O'Malley's fishwife's wail. "Barney, dear fellow, you're being a bit of bore," he said in one of those quiet yet commanding public-school put-downs the English can do at birth. "Dan is here at my invitation. In any event, he will not be here long. We're about to be on our way, in my car. And he has my permission to leave his in my parking space."

The look on O'Malley's puss cried out for a camera. Saying nothing, he shambled off. Melts, I suspected, was smiling behind his beard.

I parked in a spot labelled "Director," then snuggled into the Ferrari. A Testarossa, as in testosterone. It was almost as compact inside as my Mini, which is where all comparisons collapsed. But it would be a bit of a bore to describe its features. Except for its speed: 0-60 in 5.2 whiplashes. Within seconds we had slingshot on to the Upper Levels, eagle-high above West Vancouver.

"That O'Malley is—not to put too fine a point on it—a son of a bitch," Melts said delicately. "And speaking of sons of bitches, that eyrie coming up there on the left is the place Adam Graves is leasing. It's not far from the place Peter Cowan has been living in."

I'd seen the boxy brown cedar house before, half of it hanging off the mountainside, perched on stilts. "I gather Graves can afford the rent."

"Quite well-off, he is. Or, perhaps, was. He appears to be in a spot of trouble at the moment. Indeed, from what I gleaned at our meeting this morning, his finances are somewhat . . . *tenuous.*"

What was happening, he said, was that the film had already

cost fifteen million and change—and needed at least another four to five to complete. Of course, had he known Graves didn't have all the money in place, he would never have signed as director. Graves had brought the project up to British Columbia simply to take advantage of the lower Canadian dollar. He also had some hope of local silent investors, to share the risk. But they'd been gun-shy, don't you know, ever since the federal government had closed the tax-shelter loophole that once allowed them to write off all of their investment over two years. Up until a few weeks ago, Graves had been on the verge of raising cash through blind pools on the stock exchange next door in Alberta. As Melts explained them, these were junior capital pools that allowed new companies to issue stock on the exchange without owning any assets or disclosing a business plan. Then the Alberta Securities Commission got tough on a couple of hopeful film producers who'd tried to circumvent the already lax regulations. Not surprisingly, Graves became nervous and aborted that scheme. His most recent idea was to take over a shell company on the Vancouver exchange and sell shares in the film. In a horribly perverse way, Melts said, the publicity about Bobbi Flynn's death was helping him.

"You don't seem terrifically upset by all this financial fina-gling," I said. "Doesn't it affect the future of this picture?"

"The truth? Certainly, if he founders, the picture goes down with him. But I would be lying if I said anything other than I would welcome the expiration of this abominable venture. Since Bobbi . . . *died,* my head and heart have not been in it. We'd great hopes for this one, all of us, but it seemed benighted from the beginning. Tensions between Burt and that oaf Cowan, between Graves and Bobbi . . . "

"Between you and Bobbi."

The Ferrari slowed slightly. "Ah, quite right. Bucketsful, as it turned out. Truth to tell, I was infatuated with her at the first. She was the most . . . *comely* creature I'd experienced in years."

"And did you experience her?"

"You're nothing if not direct. We had a brief thing, actually. The police were very persistent about that, so it's an open book. It also hardly qualifies as a secret, I'm sure, that Bobbi spurned me subsequently."

"When she began seeing Georgia West."

"I'm not so certain it was such direct cause and effect. But the ultimate outcome was that, yes, we no longer spent any time together off the set. A fact which caused me some grief."

"Not enough, though, to be vengeful."

"If you're asking me, did I kill Bobbi Flynn, my answer is, no, of course not. If you're asking, did I have the opportunity, it's remotely possible, given that I didn't spend the entire evening in question at the dailies. But my reaction to your asking is anger. I may be a silly fool about romance, but I'm not a murderer."

"Do you have any idea who may be, in this case?"

We picked up speed, heading down the hill to Horseshoe Bay and the ferry terminal. The sportscar veered off and up again on the road to Squamish. "I'm not a betting man, but if I were, I'd put my shekels on Georgia West's pimp . . . . Lord, I always find that view exquisite!"

He was looking out over *ahh*-inspiring Howe Sound, its islands and the rearing mountains that, through the rain, were cutouts of black velvet. The Squamish Highway parallels the sound, if that's the right way to describe a seaside mountain road that skitters madly through an endless series of zigs and zags, uphills and downs. We quickly came to the first of the signs picturing sharp little slopes with what looked like elephant droppings tumbling down them.

ROCKFALL HAZARD AREA
NO STOPPING FOR 200M

On our immediate right, the highway tucked under the crumbling cliffs, some of them ominously swathed in wire mesh. On our near left, it rimmed skinny stands of spruce and cedar and, just beyond them, a long sheer drop to the sound. Caught between the two, I thought I'd prefer the deep blue sea to the devil mountains. Those pretty bronze and silver rockfaces have been known to fall in great lumps and turn the road into an instant mortuary for cars. And in the Lions Bay subdivision up ahead, whole houses roosting on old creek beds have slid down the slopes and become giant chopsticks at the edge of the road.

None of which was bothering Bob Melts, who had obviously just taken the lead in the Stirling Moss Memorial Grand Prix.

"Tell me more about Adam Graves," I said, trying to break his trance, slow his speed, save my life.

"Fair's fair. I've told you about his financial troubles. You tell me what you learned in reading the West person's diary. Then I'll give you more about bloody Graves."

For only the third time in two days, I summed up how Georgia had chronicled her last years in her own blackly eloquent words. Though Melts winced and shook his head at the appropriate moments, it wasn't until I brought Bobbi into the picture that he eased off on the accelerator. I didn't edit for delicacy. His features, masked by the full black beard, were a blank canvas. No signs of pain, of compassion, sketched themselves on that face. Until I recounted Bobbi's humiliation of Georgia, when I saw some moisture collect at the corner of his right eye. Love unconsummated, love gone wrong.

As good a time as any to make the transition back to Graves. I prodded Melts for more background on the producer.

"In this business, Adam Graves is an ... *aberration.* The norm is either the big studio or the well-established independent. But he emerged from nowhere, relatively speaking, from a strong but undistinguished business career. Once, and once only, he drunkenly boasted that he'd read law at Harvard but never really practised."

"Law at Harvard? I thought he took business at Northwestern."

"Indeed, that too, I gather."

Melts had asked around about Graves in Los Angeles and New York film circles. Through his minor theatrical investments off Broadway, some contacts in the East had met Graves, and only that. In L.A., they knew him from his trading and flipping of office properties. But the industry gossips in the Polo Lounge and the Russian Tea Room provided Melts with nothing to unsettle him, outside of the prospective producer's womanizing. He figured, actually, that Graves' inexperience in the field would give the director on this picture more power. And when another project went into turnaround—Hollywood for deferral or death—Melts gratefully accepted this one.

How had Graves come to him? Do you know, he told me, it seemed he had Bobbi Flynn to thank for that. He'd directed her in one of the first TV movies of the week she did in branching out from her soap career. While their relationship hadn't become close, she'd trusted him to make her look better on screen than her experience and talent ever could. Graves, meanwhile, had met Bobbi at one of his elaborate parties and seemed smitten with her—although she'd insisted to Melts that he had never sullied her. Not her type. Yet, despite his fascination with her, the first-time producer was a clever enough businessman not to give her the bank when she signed with him. At that point, her first major film hadn't been released. When it was, and she became your classic overnight star in the Hollywood firmament, she'd gone after Graves for more money.

"Here we are. Almost there," Melts said, nodding to an abrupt hump on the skyline ahead. It was the granite monolith of the Chief, a favourite of rock climbers. A minute or two later, just this side of the peak, we were turning into the parking lot for Shannon Falls Provincial Park. I looked at my watch. Less than thirty minutes—I'd never done the drive faster than forty.

Behind lofty evergreen, we could make out the slender cataract of the ragged, frothing falls. The water tumbles eleven hundred feet, virtually straight down the mountainside. The local Squamish Indians had a legend that a sea serpent they called Say-noth-ka created the spillway for the falls by cork-screwing up and down the cliff. A more recent story, that the water's pure enough for brewers to collect and make beer with, is no longer true.

It would be the setting for one of the last scenes Bob Melts had to shoot. The fitful rain had discouraged the tourists today. The day after tomorrow, cast and crew would be here. Now he wanted to walk through the action himself and with an assistant. Shrouded in yellow slickers he'd brought along, we ambled through moss-wrapped maples and cedars tall and true enough for totem poles. Past a wooden replica of a water wheel. Up a twisting log-and-plank bridge that took us to a couple of figures in the same hooded raingear.

They greeted us, Melts introducing me to Jack, his second-unit director, and Andy, his DP. Director of Photography, I figured out later. No mention of what I was doing there. The next hour was like being a guest at an Esperanto convention. Occasionally I could pick out words and phrases that sounded exactly like English. But they were strung apart by so much industry jargon—scrims, sticks, 5297 film—that I began to tune out as I huddled under a fat-leafed maple. The trio was considering infinite variations of camera set-ups and angles for a climactic scene where a bad guy's body would bump inelegantly down the falls. A rockpile rose at their base, and the cameramen had climbed the fence separating it from the public and were clambering around the boulders in rubber boots. Melts stood more securely below them, singing out suggestions.

By now, my suggestion was for all of us to get the hell out of the rain and go home. I was saved from the embarrassment of voicing it by the finality of Melts' call: "That will do nicely, chaps." Seemingly satisfied, he led the way back down the bridge to the parking lot, where we stripped off our slickers and he exchanged a few more words with Andy.

Back in the Ferrari, he said, "Under normal circumstances, that little session would have consumed two to three more hours. It's a measure of my impatience with this project that we are leaving so precipitously. Would you care to share some warmth?" He pulled a silver flask from his glove compartment and offered me a swallow. Dark rum, straight.

"Thanks. Incidentally, Bob, my two daughters have been harassing me to see a real movie being made. Would it be a terrific inconvenience if I brought them up here for a quick look round on Saturday?"

"Not at all. It's a big location, and a public one. So long as you don't raise their hopes about what they might be seeing."

If anything, the return trip was even quicker. But time enough for me to evoke some of his feelings about Barney O'Malley "There have been some absolutely top drawer examples of the ad/pub man," he began. "Fellows like Hy Smith, who was at United Artists through thin as well as a thick, and who handled himself with a certain dignity. And then there are the outright flacks, whose morals are so contemptible they would nauseate their own mothers—if they hadn't already sold them for thirty pieces of good press.

"O'Malley is, unhappily, a wretched example of the latter. He is notorious for his smarmy dealings with the Hollywood movie media, which in the past haven't been exactly celebrated for a sense of righteousness. There was the occasion when he was flacking a particularly abysmal movie and flew in a ragtag junket of small-town print reporters from the Midwest. He wined and dined them for three days, which is what's expected. He supplied some of them with hookers, which is not entirely *un*expected. Then he overreached even himself. Apparently with only a slight prodding, he introduced several of these naive hicks to the multifarious wonders of cocaine. You know the denouement: one of them died of an overdose. It was hushed up, of course, but everybody in the business knew. And he was unofficially blacklisted, which only intensified his drunkenness."

"So how would he wind up in what at least started as a respectable film project?"

"Principally, Adam Graves' inexperience. But more than that, Barney is one of those insidious human beings who can spot a character weakness, no matter how many fathoms deep it's buried. Somebody told me he sprang from a big Irish-American family. One where the father presented a sober, back-slapping self to the world—and then, in the privacy of his own home, drank like a demon and beat his wife and children like hell."

Melts fell silent as he began to pass a sluggish logging truck near the crest of a hill. I had a little trouble concentrating myself when an oncoming tourist bus materialized suddenly. We slipped in front of the truck with a second to spare.

"Barney knows what people are capable of," he continued, unruffled. "He knows how to show two very distinctive faces to two different audiences—the perfect trait for his trade. He's also a grand master at insinuating himself, at becoming indispensable. He does for people. There's a marvellous Yiddish word for his kind: *makher*, someone who makes things happen. A fixer. A movie set, you must realize, is a pressure cooker. People are out of their usual element and become outlandishly grateful for even the smallest favours that make their lives easier."

"Such as?"

"I'd be quite astonished if it wasn't Barney O'Malley who arranged to get the gun for Graves, which Burt Gold then somehow retrieved and used to threaten Adam. And, although I hadn't recalled it until this moment, I did hear—secondhand, mind—that Barney had been supplying Burt with tranquillizers for his nervous condition."

16

Paydirt

❖❖

Whenever my optimism bubbles over, Nadia figures it's her duty to deflate it by quoting one of her mother's endless old Ukrainian sayings. Roughly translated, this one goes: "Praise the day in the evening." This Friday morning had begun sweetly enough to encourage some inflated hope for the rest of the day. Nadia herself was responsible for my mood. She'd called to say that her better idea for my future had borne fruit. If I agreed, Dan Rudnicki was now a freelancer for the *Sun*, helping her on a day-to-day basis to investigate the continuing scandal surrounding *The Empty Gun*. She had managed a rate of only $175 a day, much less than I made at TransWorld, half what Graves had been paying. The tradeoff, she pointed out, was that my new employer was somewhat less scuzzy.

"But what would the *Sun* management say if their new employee was just a little bit scuzzy?" I described Bob Melts' character assassination of Barney O'Malley, my own suspicions about the man, and the mere outlines of my mildly devious plan to find out more about him.

"Does any of this include breaking and entering? Because if it does, Dan, I can't countenance it. If you ever got caught, my managing editor would be on my tail so fast."

"Then I won't give you any details. But I can promise you I won't be breaking in anywhere."

We agreed I'd report back tonight or tomorrow morning. Nadia would be making her own more conventional checks on Graves. I told her to confirm he'd taken law at Harvard. She had two items of interest for me. Burt Gold had been transferred to the much more agreeable psych ward at the university hospital. And the police had mounted a major search for Donny Breen.

"Missing the girls?" she asked.

"Yep. Though I'm glad to have them safely away on an island while somebody like Breen is off his leash. I'm picking them up at the ferry tomorrow."

First, call Cypress Studios and ask for O'Malley in the flat north-end Winnipeg voice of my boyhood. One finger resting on the disconnect button, ready to click off in case he actually came on the line.

"I'm sorry, Mr. O'Malley is tied up in a meeting. May I take a message?"

"I'll call back. Do you know when he'll be free?"

"He said to hold all calls till eleven."

I had a couple of hours, guaranteed. Next, drive down to the Pan Pacific, where Melts had told me O'Malley and most of the out-of-town crew were staying. The hotel is part of a classy downtown waterfront complex. It looks like a cross between a schooner under full sail and an ocean liner—a jumbo version of the glossy Alaska cruise ships that tie up alongside the hotel all summer. A trade and convention centre sits under a roofline of five fabric sails. The Pan Pacific rises to form the bridge of the complex. The whole thing is owned, like so many other key local properties, by Asian interests.

Stopping in at a nearby florist, I ordered their cheapest bouquet, addressed it to Barney O'Malley and arranged immediate delivery. Dancing through the rain to a pay phone next door, I called the hotel.

"Can you connect me with the front desk, please?" My plummiest accent. "Hello, with whom am I speaking? Mr. Raymond? Mr. Raymond, I'm calling on behalf of one of your guests, Barney O'Malley. I'm Mr. O'Malley's personal assistant. Mr. O'Malley has asked me to arrange a small staff meeting in his room this morning . . . No, it's only a couple of people so we don't need the board room . . . No, we don't need anything. Well, maybe some coffee and extra cups. You're very kind. But why I'm calling, Mr. Raymond, is that Mr. O'Malley wanted to have some flowers to brighten up the room . . . No, no, it's all arranged. I'm having some sent over. In fact, they should be arriving in the next few minutes. Will you make sure a bellman takes them up immediately? Now, one more thing. Mr. O'Malley is already on his way and he didn't leave me his room number. Can you . . . Of course, I understand. It's a very commendable policy not to give out room numbers over the phone. I could be anyone. That's no problem, I'll call him from the house phone when I arrive. Thank you for all your trouble, Mr. Raymond."

Thanks for nothing, Mr. Raymond. Better hop over there like a rabbit in heat.

I rode the escalator up to the lobby. Enormous as it is, it's dwarfed by a sky-scraping ceiling, several storeys high, that gives the reception area all the intimacy of a shopping mall. A couple of minutes' unobtrusive wait, and there came my florist's delivery man. Good, he's going to the front desk.

They're calling over a bellman. Nods of head all around. Bellman heads for the elevator, with me on his heels.

"Could you hold the door, please?" He punched 8. "Oh, that's my floor, too . . . Mmm, some lucky lady, looks like."

The young bellman, wearing a badge identifying him as Bruce, looked down at the box of flowers and said, "Naw, they're going to some guy."

I let Bruce lead me off on the eighth floor. Hesitated to see where he was heading, then followed a casual distance behind. "I say," I called out after he'd knocked on 820 and paused before letting himself in. "Those flowers couldn't be for Mr. O'Malley, could they?"

"Yeah. O'Malley."

"Well, that's a coincidence. They arrived in good time for the meeting." I began to walk into what was a two-room suite.

He stood just inside the door like a column. "You're not O'Malley. I know O'Malley."

Strike one. "No, I'm his assistant. He's expecting me. I guess he got held up in traffic. You don't mind if I just come in and get things ready for the meeting."

"Sorry," he said, shaking his head. "We got strict orders not to let anybody in the rooms when paying guests aren't there."

Two.

I muttered something about how inconvenient this all was, and how Mr. O'Malley would be terribly upset about not having things in apple-pie order for the meeting. Peering around him at the unmade bed in the separate bedroom, I said, "At the very least, could you have the maid come in immediately and tidy up?" He shrugged agreement and picked up the room phone to call housekeeping.

Base hit.

I returned to the elevator, went one floor down, waited there a few minutes, then rode it back to the eighth. The door to 820 was open. The over-efficient Bruce had gone. In his place a young Filipino maid was making up the bed.

I strode in and smiled at her. "Wonderful, wonderful! If you could possibly hurry it up, my dear. Expecting some friends in any moment." Her surprise seemed to be based on my sudden appearance, not any suspicion that I was an impostor. Opening a dresser drawer, I rummaged through it as if I'd misplaced my wallet. "No need to do the bathroom now, if you don't mind. Perhaps I can call you later, after our meeting."

Whisking her out, I quickly decided priorities. I could leave the search of his personal effects for later, if there was time. I headed straight for the bank of filing folders I'd seen on the table in the sitting room. Perhaps twenty of them, labelled alphabetically, beginning with Advertising, and then running through various administrative headings and the names of the major players in *The Empty Gun.* So Cowan was there, Flynn, Gold, Graves, Melts. I went right to Bobbi's file. A press release dated last year, O'Malley prose proclaiming her Hollywood's Most Vibrant and Vivacious New Star. Assorted clippings about her from magazines and newspapers—and that was it.

Disappointed, I delved into the other personal files. They were virtually identical, dammit, filled only with official bios and the other backup material he'd used to compose his releases. The administrative folders—Advertising, Media Contacts, Postproduction—took a lot more time but yielded as little. No wonder he felt comfortable leaving these lying around.

I had no idea what I was looking for. Some hints, maybe, about the man's character, or lack of it. The faint imprint of a crucial phone number on a notepad. O'Malley's full written confession to both murders. I tried not to reflect on that stupid proverb about praising the day too early. The sight of all those files had raised unreasonable hopes.

Have to settle down, start looking through his drawers and cupboards, his clothes and suitcases. Lord, the man's a swine. I should have let the maid stay and clean the bathroom. Towels on the floor, hair all over the tub. Nothing in the medicine chest but bottles of pills, likely most of them for the industrial-strength hangovers he must suffer.

A drawer in the sitting-room confirmed that hunch. His private bar, a case and a half of Glenlivet. The other drawers held hotel-issue books, magazines, a Gideon, whose pages hid no scrap of paper more interesting than a particularly gross pinup from *Hustler*. The hall cupboard had the usual coats and jackets, which I frisked painstakingly in search of The Elusive Clue That Would Break This Case Wide Open.

Thirty-five minutes already. The bedroom. I fastidiously removed every item from a dresser jammed with O'Malley's elephant-sized shirts and shorts, tasteless jewellery and a dozen clown-like bowties. Got to be thorough. Behind the pictures. Under the bed. Hey, maybe twice lucky: I pulled the bed away from the wall. Nothing fell to the floor. Where else? The cupboard. It was even more disgusting than my daughters'. Buried under a haystack of clothes were three suitcases. The clothing, first.

The rapping on the door sounded like hailstones on my head.

And had the same effect. My mind froze.

More knocking.

Nowhere to hide.

"Room service." Bruce the bellman. With the coffee I'd cavalierly ordered from the front desk.

The door handle was twisting open. "Hold on!" I said in a crummy impression of O'Malley's whiskey-worn voice. I slipped into the bathroom and called out as I was closing the door, "Bring it in." Then, muffled: "Take care of you later."

"Thanks, Mr. O'Malley." The door eased shut.

I emerged slowly from the bathroom and sat on the edge of the bed, wondering if Woodward and Bernstein had ever rifled a hotel room. No, it was the other way around, some bad guys breaking into a suite at the Watergate that started them investigating the whole Nixon administration.

Time to get going. I patted down O'Malley's dirty clothes as gingerly as possible. Pulled out one suitcase. Empty. The second had an aromatic hoard of dirty socks. The third was just as light. Tossing it on the bed, I tried to open it. Sealed with a three-number combination lock. What did I promise Nadia? No breaking in. Nothing about entering.

One of the most common number codes people use for suitcases is the last three digits of the year they were born in. O'Malley would be about fifty-five. Try 934. Still locked. Maybe it was just the booze that made him look that old. Work my way up the years: 5, 6…939 did it. He was only fifty?

Barney O'Malley had carefully locked his suitcase to conceal a clutch of skin magazines. A special kind: with nude little girls in sexual poses, pre-adolescents, sometimes smiling seductively, sometimes in bondage and looking terrified.

No, not only that. Below the magazines lay another file folder, this one labelled Miscellaneous. It too contained press clippings. But these were different. I pulled out a notepad and started making notes.

The first paper-clipped batch was mostly pages photocopied from medical journals. They shared a single theme that seemed to be of great interest to O'Malley: the artificial penis. All but one of the articles reported on the incredible lengths female-to-male transsexuals went through to get a phony phallus—one woman had thirty-three plastic-surgery operations. And how seldom they were satisfied with the results. The scarring was horrendous, the organs looked awkward, and sexual function was disappointing or nonexistent.

The variations in building material for a constructed penis seemed boundless. Inserting a permanent semi-rigid prosthesis. Implanting acrylics. Grafting bone from a leg or cartilage from a woman's own rib—Eve's rib, you could say. But the article with the most text underlined and circled was one from *Science News* describing a procedure that was supposed to create a more successful sculpted phallus. It used an inflatable prosthesis. The transsexual had a liquid-filled reservoir in his abdomen. Pumping a small bulb in the scrotum filled two cylinders in the penis, causing a kind of erection—and allowing intercourse, though not always orgasm. The journal, a little overexuberantly, called this "a more aesthetic and sexually functioning artificial penis."

The second batch was brief newspaper stories, longer magazine pieces, and a transcript from the TV series *20/20*, all dealing with a drug that had become the most frequently prescribed sleeping pill in the world. It appeared to be a powerful drug—one article called it sixty times more powerful than Valium—with unexpectedly potent side effects.

The Food and Drug Administration had ruled that it should not be taken for more than 14 days. Dosage should not exceed .25 milligrams a day. And, while most people seemed to handle it well enough, the FDA warned that it could cause loss of memory, anxiety and depression.

These press reports were claiming even worse side effects. In some people, they said, it produced extreme behaviour—including hallucinations and paranoia, attempted suicide and, in at least one case, murder. The TV transcript documented the story of a Utah woman who killed her beloved mother with eight gunshots, then placed a birthday card in her hand. Charged with second-degree murder, the daughter was sent to a psychiatric hospital. The diagnosis was mental impairment from this sleeping pill, which she'd been taking under doctor's orders for months. The prosecution dropped all charges against her.

Some countries had questioned the strength of the common dosage, and Holland had taken the pill off the market after complaints about its side effects. In North America, despite the controversy, it seemed to be still quite legal.

The drug was called Halcion.

As in "Oh, these are still halcyon days."

❖❖

17

Praise
the Day

❖❖

Young Bruce was hanging about the lobby,
waiting for the next guest to charm. Approaching him with my
most winning expression, I fished out a fiver and said, plum-
mily, "Thanks, young man, they're all settled in there with Mr.
O'Malley, and most appreciative of the coffee." Which I had
just dumped down the bathroom sink before leaving the
thermos and tray of cups outside someone else's room.

"You seem to know Mr. O'Malley," I continued, extracting
a cigarette and offering him one, which he reluctantly declined.

"Yeah. He's an okay guy." Heavy tipper.

"You've most likely heard about all the problems we're
having with the movie we're making. The tragic death of Bobbi
Flynn."

He nodded, looking a little more interested now. I told him
there was a bit of an on-going discussion with the police over

this unfortunate affair. We were determined to clear it up once and for all. And although it had been a while, we were wondering if he happened to know which bellmen were on duty the night of her murder and who would have brought Mr. O'Malley's late dinner to him.

Sure he knew. He already told his boss, who told the police. And it was? Him, of course. He was on graveyard that night. Well, did he recall any of the circumstances—such as exactly what he'd brought Mr. O'Malley and about what time he'd delivered it to him.

A shrug. "It's always the same thing that time of night. Corn beef and cabbage, and a bucket of ice. I can't remember the exact time now, but like I told my boss, I left it for him just after midnight."

"What do you mean—left it for him? Wasn't he in the room?"

"Oh yeah, he was there, but room service said I hadda knock once. And if there was no answer, that meant we shouldn't disturb him, just leave it at the door. You know, he sometimes, uh, entertains late. You gotta be sort of *discreet* in this job."

And no, he hadn't told the police about leaving the meal at the door. He was on holiday when they came round asking, so his boss checked out the room-service records for them. After Bruce returned to work, he just confirmed the time for his boss, who called the cops back.

❖❖

So, I told myself on the drizzly drive out to the university hospital, Barney O'Malley could have done exactly what I did. On the night of Bobbi Flynn's murder, he could have called from outside the hotel—room service wouldn't necessarily notice or recall if he was phoning from his suite or not. Bruce had brought up the meal, knocked once as requested, figured the randy guest was entertaining again, and left the meal outside the door. You gotta be discreet. Luckily for Barney O'Malley, no one had thought to ask if Bruce actually handed it to him in person. And obviously no one on staff had paid any attention to how long the tray had sat in the corridor.

During the term, UBC is a small city of thirty thousand. With exams over, most of the students had dispersed. But the Health Sciences hospital, on a pleasant patch of the central campus, was keeping busy, perhaps with post-exam students. Visitors were lined up at the psychiatric ward's reception desk. The wait gave me a chance to choose from a full menu of reasons why the hospital should allow me to see Burt Gold, none of which held any water.

Was I a relative? a nice nurse finally asked me.

She couldn't see the family resemblance?

She didn't know Mr. Gold that well. I could visit him now in the common room, although there was someone else with him, a friend from the movie company.

The ward was attractive, restful, a world apart from River-view.

Jennie's surprised smile cheered me even more. "What are you doing—?" we both began. Sitting beside Gold on a plump couch, she explained that she'd just tied up the very last of Bobbi's business affairs and was saying goodbye to Burt. " . . . who's looking very well, don't you think?"

He was. A bit more weight on the body, a lot less languor in the eyes. Eyes that were now looking at me intently, as if they'd never seen me before. Which was probably true.

Jennie was looking well too, in Girbaud jeans and another woolly sweater. I was quick to reassure her that I was no longer working for the same fellow—unidentified, for Gold's sake—and that my new employer was the *Sun*. We not only wanted to make sure Burt's name continued to stay cleared, we also wanted to see the real murderer arrested. Jennie put in an ambiguous plug for me with Burt: "A decent man doing a grotty job." She was staring at me the way I had at her when we'd met. How could I have suspected she was anything but a genuine Jennie.

"Burt," I began, "I have some fresh, and pretty disturbing, information to pass on and check with you. Are you up to talking about it?"

"I'm . . . " He was still tired, Jennie said, and sometimes confused, but if it was important, I should mention it. Burt nodded slowly.

I gave him as much background as I thought he could take in one gulp, adding the occasional elaboration for Jennie. I didn't complicate things by talking about Georgia West's death. But I did refer to her diary, which piqued Jennie's interest. Then the collective suspicion about Barney O'Malley, his odd relationship with Adam Graves, and the alibi that had just burst.

"But the most important fact, the reason I'm here, is hard to comprehend. I think it's possible O'Malley is guilty of murder. But even if he is, I can't understand a man who could then cold-bloodedly frame someone else for it. And I believe that's exactly what Barney O'Malley did to you, Burt. Do you remember telling me . . . it doesn't matter if you do. I saw you at Riverview when you were much less well. You said something funny to me then, something about halcyon days. Do you know what you meant?"

He was slow to speak, and when he did his voice was weak, a Rip Van Winkle trying out his vocal cords after twenty years' slumber. "I—I did? I did say that?" He gently shook his head. "I don't know . . . But '*halcyon* days' . . . Sh-Shakespeare . . . Halcyon, halcyon. *Halcion.* Uh-huh. Maybe I meant Halcion. It's a sleeping pill. I've been taking it to get through the night . . . Or, I was. They said they wouldn't give it to me anymore."

"Who did?"

"The people . . . here, when I asked for it."

"But how did you get it in the first place?"

"One—one day, Barney gave me some. I couldn't sleep, I

was worried about—about the script. And he said he had something that would help."

"Do you remember how many you took at a time?"

"Barney told me . . . he said to take three pills, to make sure it worked." Triple the recommended dosage.

It took a while, but with Jennie's help we worked it out, using dramatic events in the filming of *The Empty Gun* as guideposts. O'Malley had first given Burt the Halcion about five weeks before he exploded into Graves' office brandishing the gun. And it had been only about three weeks, Jennie estimated, before she'd begun noticing a striking change in Burt's personality. Such as the time he'd insisted Johnny Carson was including a secret code in his monologue to help Burt revise his script.

Jennie was giving me a look—not of fondness this time, but of warning. "Okay, Burt, I think that's enough for now," I said. "But I'd like to tell the police about all this, and you may be getting a visit from an Inspector Rusk. He's a decent man . . . doing a grotty job." Which got me an elbow in the back. "Oh, and one more thing, Burt. When I was with you last, you quoted a line from a movie that starts: 'A man needs a little madness . . . ' Where's it from? It's been driving me crazy ever since."

" ' . . . or else he never dares cut the rope and be free.' Anthony Quinn. *Zorba the Greek.*"

Jennie gave Burt a long goodbye embrace, then joined me in the hall. "If you cabbed it here," I suggested, "I can double you back on my trusty steed."

"I'd like that, O perfect gentle knight."

"Let me just use that pay phone for a minute." Phil Rusk was not thrilled to hear from me, especially when told I was now working for the *Sun.* But the professional in him listened to the shorthand version of my case against O'Malley. How he knew more about Donny Breen than he should. How the diary referred to a transsexual B. which, strange as it seemed, could mean Barney. How the hotel bellman had remembered leaving the food outside O'Malley's door. Finally, my talk with a much improved Burt Gold at the hospital—"Who did you say you were this time, Rudnicki?" Rusk wondered, in his only interruption. And how O'Malley had urged Burt to take a high dose of Halcion, whose documented side effects include paranoia and violence.

"That doesn't prove O'Malley knew about those effects," Rusk said.

"He knew. I have it on good authority that, back at his hotel, he has a suitcase full of hard facts detailing exactly what the abuse of Halcion can do."

"I won't even ask on whose authority, Rudnicki."

"So will you be doing anything with any of this?"

No reply. Probably taking a long drag on a pungent cigar. "Some of it is circumstantial, some of it depends on the testimony of a man still considered mentally ill. But I will have somebody look at it, when we can. At the moment we are neck-deep in another morass, the pursuit of a much more likely suspect by the name of Donald Breen. A name that, perhaps even you have noticed, also bears the initial letter B. It is far better to have one known madman in hand before worrying about a possible second in the bush."

"I won't even ask on whose authority you know that, Inspector."

❖❖

Jennie was kind enough not to comment on the Mini.

As we headed to Marine Drive, the scenic route, I asked where we were going—had she eaten? No, and she'd invite me to her place, but it was stripped of everything but her suitcases. She was flying to New York tomorrow. So soon. I proposed having a bite, and talking, at my house. With the kids away, it would be quiet. That would be fine.

We were skating around, supported by a surface tension,

168

not yet prepared to break through the ice and wallow in what we had felt for one another the first time. I was answering her questions about Georgia and O'Malley as we passed by the beaches of Spanish Banks and Locarno, where dogs were walking people in the rain. The subject was Breen as we pulled up to the high old house with the big porch hidden behind the laurel hedge on Kits Point.

By unspoken consent, we fell silent as I took her coat and motioned to the livingroom. She walked in, stopped, gazed around, absorbing details. The slab-stone fireplace dominating one corner. The battered Steinway upright. The wall of books, records and videos. The tall stained glass in the centre of the bay window looking out over the front yard and its raffish, overgrown cherry tree. Nothing designer-beautiful, but homey with a pile of *Archie* comics and a pair of Keds. Whose owners were pictured in a framed photograph on the mantel, a portrait Jennie was now studying with a smile.

She pointed to the diningroom, and I waved her in. Not much there beyond my grandmother's walnut table and buffet. The kitchen a little more interesting, with its fat iron farm stove beside a sleek dull gas range. I led her through the hall and up the stairs to a tongue-and-groove sunroom in back, still cold in spring. She peeked in at the girls' rooms, and laughed, probably at her own young self. Then we were outside my bedroom.

Still not speaking, Jennie cocked her head to me and looked quizzical. My answering nod could mean Yes, this is my bedroom. We both knew it didn't. She crossed the threshold and I was lost. Approaching her from behind, I put my hands gently on her waist. She turned and sank herself into my body. I held tight as she lifted her lips to mine. We were like that for an eon, an instant.

When she smiled up at me, I said, "For one wretched moment a long time ago, I thought it just barely possible that you could be Georgia's baffling B. A transsexual."

She pushed me softly down on the bed. Pulled her sweater off slowly, standing there for a moment of my admiration. Stepped out of her jeans, held them high and let them fall to the floor. Reached back and undid her bra. And, with her right pinkie, hooked the side of her red panties and, leisurely, slid them down her legs and kicked them away.

A longer moment, of anticipation. Everything was so small and perfectly formed, like a cameo.

She tumbled on me.

We took turns undressing me, in between oases of caressing and kissing, discovering and exploring, with fingers and lips and tongues that did everything but speak. The room was darkening as we rested. I rose to find some food and returned with red wine and paté on crackers whose crumbs we ignored the rest of the evening.

I fell asleep praising the day.

❖❖

18

On
Location

❖❖

When I awoke about seven the next morning, the bed was empty.

It was a trusty steed, the note said. *It transported me to places I would like to return to, someday. But not now, not soon. I must go pick up my life in New York, perhaps remake it, as I try to forget the pain I'm leaving behind here. You helped me forget for a little—a long—while. I needed this, needed you for one special night.*

Jennie

Her phone was probably disconnected. I didn't try. For a couple of hours, I lay there feeling discarded, wronged, self-righteous. Until I realized I'd needed Jennie, and used her, just as much as she had me. To escape the fear and tumult of the last few days. To collaborate on a death-defying act. And eventually I smiled at the thought of how pleasurably, how finally, she'd convinced me of her true gender.

The smile soon faded to black. Why does my dark night of

the soul always descend first thing in the morning? I began wondering what I had convinced Jennie of. If I wasn't in fact the perfect, gentle knight of her fancy, who was I? Don Quixote? But even he'd had the *chutzpah* to ride out and do battle with dragons, however phantom. Until recently, I'd been doing battle with nothing more challenging than insurance cheats.

Not doing is as definite an act, with its own inescapable consequences, as doing. Philosophy 101—or did I just make that up? For the past ten years I'd been trapped in a self-woven web, letting my life happen to me like a victim. Since Sarah had died, the only thing I'd purposefully *been* was a father. My life was a mess of pottage, whatever the hell that is. My career—a word Phil Rusk wouldn't dignify it with—had begun as happenstance and survived as a trade-off of security against ambition. My love life was about as shocking as Shevchenko's, and he was neutered before he knew what to do with it. Two affairs in five years, neither of them persisting past that fabled six-month mark where human reason is finally supposed to surmount animal passion. Somewhere in my right brain there always lingered at least the abstract *notion* of Nadia and me. A notion she never wanted to realize by re-creating the galvanic coupling of our college days.

I'm a slow study. The personal significance of the events of the week past were only beginning to trickle into my consciousness. Georgia's murder, Breen's attack on me, O'Malley's attempt to frame Burt with a frightening drug—life was getting a little too real and earnest. I'd fallen into security work, and its encouragement of play-acting, its potential for excitement, had appealed to the little boy in me. But now I was having to grow up awful fast and make some Adult Decisions. Such as, did I want to pursue this fledgling career as a freelance private investigator. Maybe it was just a more dramatic umbrella to work under while I walked the same tightrope I'd been on with TransWorld. But without the safety net of a regular paycheque.

The trade did seem to suit my temperament. The chameleon, reflecting back to people what they wanted to see, what I wanted them to see to get what I wanted. A smidgeon of the actor, the professional liar who puts on masks and tells stories that may not be the truth but are not exactly lies. All in a good cause, of course. No suggestion of venality, no willingness to sell out for sordid motives. Oh no, my motives were forever as pure as the driven snow —which these days is laced with acid.

The job, even when I had Jimmy Wright as a boss, always offered the illusion of independence. Being on a stake-out, doing a locate, posing as an employee in a store being stolen blind—they were all solo performances. The director was offstage and, once you were up there alone in the spotlight, you could interpret, adapt, make the part your own. Working for myself, becoming a one-man show, would mean only more of that freedom. Including the freedom to fall flat on my prat in public. But I was beginning to realize that the insecurity of true independence might be more soul-satisfying than the shackles of a salaried job.

The phone rang, thank God. I grabbed it to hear the message I'd recorded on my machine last night. Played back, my whispery voice was thick with wine and other intoxicants.

"Hold on, it's me," I broke in.

"God, you should re-record that message, Dan. It sounds like you're dying."

"G'morning, Nadge. You're up. Bright. Early."

"And bursting to hear everything that happened yesterday."

Everything. Yes, well, I said, the most relevant things were that Burt Gold confirmed O'Malley had conned him into taking triple doses of Halcion for more than a month. That I had then called Phil Rusk, who seemed interested but not overexcited, given the case that was building against Breen. And that I therefore intended to confront Barney O'Malley myself, to allow him at least the formality of defending himself before we went to press with any charges.

173

Terrific! When? Nadia asked. Today, if she'd join me and help keep an eye on the kids at Shannon Falls. I was collecting Esther and Larissa at Horseshoe Bay about noon and driving straight on to the location.

The next call, as I dined on day-old microwaved porridge, was my father. Sorry that he couldn't pick up his granddaughters, but wanting to bring some dinner for them before he took off to go salmon fishing with his pals. A fresh pot of *Kapusnyak*, the cabbage soup that made the girls croon and gave me gas. He'd be over in ten minutes. It was more like five, enough time for me to dress but not to do my toilette.

Much as it would shock him, I decided to confront my father about my future by being candid about the present. "Dad," I said as he was finding a place in the fridge for the soup, "I haven't told you I quit my job with TransWorld. I've been working as a freelance investigator. And I haven't confided in you about what kind of case I've been involved in." I followed up with a fast but factual recital of the assault and battery, the death and deceit of the last few days. No dreadful details spared.

He was thunderstruck. "You quit your job?" he said. "Danylo, where's your next paycheque coming from? What about the girls?"

"Dad, that's not the point. Anyway, the *Sun* has hired me under contract."

"Well, I'm happy for that. I'm also happy you weren't hurt any worse. Maybe you can tell me all about it when I get back. Mike and Ivan are over at the house, waiting."

When Nadia arrived, I was smoking the last of three Craven "A"s. If she noticed my open rebellion, she didn't comment. She had that look I see on her face when she's about to wield her column like a bludgeon and nail some unsuspecting sinner to the wall. "I'm delighted with this development about old Barney," she said as we drove to the ferry in my Mini. "Frankly, I haven't been able to get anything particularly juicy

174

on Adam Graves. I have a freelancer in New York researching his business career there, and another in Cambridge checking on his time at Harvard. From this end, I couldn't find anyone by his name who graduated from law school in the mid- to late-sixties, when he might have been there. There was a Charles Graves much earlier and a Brenda Graves in '66. Peter Cowan, now he's another story. A friend on the L.A. *Times* says there've been some persistent rumours about his sexual habits. Yet nobody's willing to spell out to her exactly what his personal aberration is. When the subject comes up, there's just a whole lot of eye-rolling and head-shaking."

"Well, one man's morality is another man's perversion."

"But, after all that, I've probably been going after the wrong man. If O'Malley is a man."

She'd been working up a Saturday feature on The Movie Murders, as she was calling them with capital letters in her voice. That required background on most of the major players. She'd found, for instance, that in the early days of the movie Graves had been telling everyone in La-La Land that his picture was going to grab an Oscar. And within a few weeks of arriving in Vancouver, he'd fired the producer working under him. Perhaps he'd learned that an Academy Award goes to the person named as the producer, not the executive producer. Or perhaps he wanted hands-on control of the project.

Nadia had dredged most of this out of the former producer, who also had interesting thoughts about Peter Cowan. He suggested that because the ageing veteran actor had been jealous of his upstart female co-star, they'd had more than the odd difference of opinion Cowan mentioned to me. And he discounted Cowan's statement that Burt Gold had shown signs of a severe nervous breakdown *before* Bobbi's murder. Burt hadn't been sleeping well then, but he was still quite sane.

"Maybe O'Malley had something on Cowan," I mused as we drove down the hill to Horseshoe Bay.

For the first time in days, it wasn't raining. With the sun

shimmering on its white hull, the little ferry from Bowen was a wedding cake on the water. The girls were almost the first off. They looked fresh, smelled sweet. Esther dropped her pack-sack and violin case and theatrically flung her arms around me as if it had been one year, not one week. Nadia received the same explosive hello. Larissa hung back for a moment, almost shyly, then let herself be embraced, resting her head on my shoulder. I pushed us apart gently and gave her a patient, open, loving look. She smiled indulgently, then took Nadia's hand and led her away for a moment.

"Dad, I made you something," Esther said, digging into her pack and flourishing a piece of burlap dangling from a drift-wood stick that hung from a piece of coloured yarn.

"That's great, S.T. What is it?"

It was, of course, a hanger for my cuff links and tie clips, neither of which I own.

"That looks like a lot of work. How did you find time?"

Larissa—back now after her little talk with Nadia—took over, as she often did, to explain in her big-sister tone. The music part of the camp was strictly the morning and they had crafts and outdoor activities in the afternoon. "Like orienteer-ing. You know what that is, don't you, Dad?"

"Finding your way around China?"

The ritual groan from all three of them. "It's when you go in teams and find your way through the woods with a map and compass. We did it a couple of days, and it was a blast. Our team won."

"You guys cheated," Esther said.

"Listen, you little hippie, you couldn't even read the map."

Too much togetherness. I broke up the impending brawl by announcing that, instead of heading straight home, we were about to watch a movie being made. They cheered, wanting to know whom they'd be seeing, and cheered again when I mentioned Peter Cowan, a name they knew from his TV reruns as a secret agent.

We picked up some fish and chips and squeezed the kids into the car with their packs. Between bites, they performed a dramatic dialogue about their entire week as the Mini bumped over those stretches of the mountain highway pockmarked with scars from fallen rocks. In some places, I had to swerve around watermelon-sized boulders that had somersaulted down the rain-weakened cliffs in a sea of stones. Sportscars on their way to Whistler, the ski and summer resort, hung on my tail, impatient for the few spots where the road widened into an uphill passing lane.

Fully loaded, my excuse for a car set a new time for the Squamish track. Fifty minutes later, as we approached the falls, I couldn't see the parking lot for the semis and panel trucks of the movie crew. A Mountie in those natty yellow-striped navy pants was waving away a busload of sullen-looking Japanese tourists, their cameras sheathed and impotent. When I slowed and Nadia stuck her press card out the window, he let us pull around him to a patch of grass on the verge of the lot.

Right next to a white limo where Adam Graves sat talking to someone on the far side of the back seat.

Seeing me, he lowered his window and said, belligerently, "Rinicky, what are you doing here?"

"I'm with her," I said, indicating Nadia.

"Oh, the newspaper lady." He gave her a skeletal smile.

"It's okay, Adam, I invited Dan and his kids here today." The passenger with Graves, climbing out of the car, was Bob Melts.

I introduced him to Nadia, who arranged to talk to him briefly during the afternoon. "Have you seen Barney O'Malley?" she asked. Melts hadn't, nor had Graves, who grunted, "He's supposed to be coming this afternoon. We didn't expect the media."

Crew were still yarding cable out of trucks, people were stepping in and out of mobile dressing rooms, and a group clustered around a catering van juggling coffee and paper plates abrim with scallops and salad.

❖❖

One of them was Leo Garnett, looking the stunt man in Levis and leather jacket. "Dan Rudnicki. You keep popping up like a gopher. Howareya, fella. This your family and your missus?" The Saskatchewan twang thickened with the audience. He was here to do one gag for Cowan, a fight on a rock ledge, which seemed as if it'd never get set up. So he had time to show the kids around, if they liked. Sure, I could join them, if I stuck by him and stayed out of people's way. Nadia wanted to look around by herself.

As we sauntered towards the falls, Leo said he'd heard I was no longer working for Graves. When I explained I was now under contract to the *Sun*, helping research a piece on the movie, he said, "Sounds like you're bulling the cow uphill. I don't think you'll get a helluva lot of co-operation from O'Malley, way I heard."

Melts was being helpful, I pointed out, and Nadia could handle the others. But I did want to talk to O'Malley when he arrived. "You'll be about as welcome as hail and 'hoppers," Leo remarked.

Near the fence that kept the public off the rocks, he paused and pointed to a man with a walkie-talkie. "Now, girls, that fella there is a gaffer. He makes sure the cameraman has all the things he needs in a location like this. He's the boss of the whole crew out here. And those two over there working on that big lamp, they're the key grip—he's the head technician—and his assistant, who's called a best boy. Have you got a best boy yet?" he asked Esther, who shook her head as she looked at her running shoes.

"This is swell," I said. "Now I'll finally learn what a dolly grip is."

"Hey, these girls know what that is. That's the way they hold on to their dolls." They loved seeing their old man being ribbed for a change. "Even your Dad probably knows a dolly grip's really the fella in charge of the dolly that holds the camera and lets it move smooth-like all around the set . . .

178

Then, over to the left, the ones beside the microphone on the long pole are the sound mixer and his side-kicks, the boom operator and the third man."

"Oh, I've heard his theme," I said. The banter, and just being with the kids, was washing away some of the stink of the case.

It all washed back when Leo said, "And there's a real live movie actor. Peter, have you got a minute to come over here and meet some young ladies?"

Cowan looked over casually, as if he were too busy to be bothered. When he saw the girls, he beamed his star's smile and came over, hobbling slightly. He was dressed in the same denim outfit as his stunt double. "Always delighted to meet such beautiful women," he said, taking Larissa's hand and then Esther's, in a lingering, mock-formal greeting. Somehow the scene bothered me. I closed my eyes, shutting it out.

"And you know their father."

Cowan hadn't even noticed me. "Oh, yes," he said, hand half-extended until he saw who it was. "You're still, uh . . . ?"

"Just visiting, at Bob Melt's invitation. The first time the girls have been on a location."

"Okay, Leo, you're on!" Jack, the second-unit director, interrupted our increasingly stiff encounter. Cowan took the opportunity to limp away.

"What happened to him?" I asked Leo as he was leaving.

"Bunny? Bunny says he fell in the tub and hurt his little paw."

"*Bunny* Cowan? Where does that come from?"

"Apparently, way back early in his career, he played Peter Rabbit on stage in a children's show. The monicker stuck."

❖❖

Movie-making is like security work. The waiting is always the worst. We waited as Leo and another stunt man, taller and wider, climbed the slick hill of rocks. We waited as Jack and the cameraman positioned them artistically against the backdrop of the falls. We waited as they re-positioned them. We waited as the stunt men danced through a slow-motion version of their fight, hewing to a choreography they'd obviously re-hearsed many times. We waited as the cameraman called for a couple of major changes in their steps. Finally, after forty-five minutes, the shot was ready.

"Okay, people, remember everything back of the fence is hot," Jack shouted. "Quiet, everyone, quiet! All right, this is a take. Action!"

Once the camera was rolling, it was easy to justify all the set-up. The fight went off as gracefully as a ballet in fast forward. The other stunt man surprised Leo from behind, leaping on his back and knocking him flat. Leo magically rolled out of his grip, jumped up and swung a fist. The usual barroom blows were exchanged, but this time delivered on rock slippery from the spray of the falls. Both men did a lot of scheduled sliding and falling. A minute into the duel, the villain grabbed a big branch and came at Leo. I thought for sure we were about to see a repeat of the scene in *Doublecross* where Leo drop-kicked the gun out of the bad guy's hand. Instead he surprised me by diving to the ground and hurling himself at the feet of his attacker—toppling him in a crude shoestring tackle that supposedly knocked him unconscious. End of scene.

"That, gentlemen, is a wrap," Jack said with a grin. The whole crew applauded. "Now, will someone help Peter up there and we'll get some close-ups."

Leo returned to the dressing room. The girls endured ten minutes of boredom, looking a little disillusioned that all the screen hero did was pose and mug for the camera. "Can we go look around?" Larissa asked. I decided to walk back with them and look for Barney O'Malley. "Don't go wandering off too far now," I warned. They scampered away, ignoring my cry of "Be careful!"

I spent the next twenty minutes wandering the area, meeting nobody I knew except Nadia, who hadn't seen O'Malley either. Melts had confirmed a few things I'd already told her. Graves had returned to the city. We were about to declare it a wrap when Esther and Larissa came running across the grassy field, hollering.

They were out of breath, barely able to talk. "Dad! Dad! There's something—" Esther began. Larissa took over. "Dad! We were orienteering just at the edge of the woods over there. Then Esther started hiding on me and when I went to find her, I found something. Someone." She broke into tears. "I think there's something the matter with him."

Nadia took Esther's hand, I grasped Larissa's, and we walked quickly over to the edge of the forest. Larissa pointed out the soft green of a maple amid the firs. "You and Esther stay right here." Nadia and I walked slowly into the trees. Some of the tall grass was matted. As I pushed underbrush aside to clear a path, we saw something. Someone, lying face down on the ground. A rivulet of blood was running from the side of his suit jacket.

I circled the bulky body to see the face.

The face of Barney O'Malley.

He was quite still.

19

Cut to
the Chase

❖❖

"**W**hat else did you see?" I asked the girls.

Larissa had wiped away the tears. "I heard something first. Like the time that dumb Frankie put the firecracker under a tin can on our porch. But I didn't pay any attention to it. Then I saw a man come out of the forest near the road. He didn't see me."

"Did you notice what he looked like?"

"No, he was going pretty fast. Just that he was fat. And I think he had reddish hair."

I gathered her and Esther in my arms, gave them a hug, then asked Nadia to stay with them while I went to find the Mountie who was directing traffic.

He wasn't there, but Leo was, eating a plate of scallops near the highway. When I quietly explained what had happened, he didn't overreact. Coolly, he said he'd just been grabbing a bite to eat when this big redheaded guy came barging out of the woods down the way a bit. Curious, Leo had walked out to the road and watched him get into a dented grey Ford parked on the shoulder. The car had turned around and taken off like a shot towards Vancouver. Just a few minutes ago.

"Ray," Leo called to a crewman eating a sandwich in the cab of his semi, "what happened to the Mountie who was here?"

"Heard he had to go off to take care of a rockfall on the road out to Whistler."

Leo told Ray to get on the pay phone near the public washrooms and call the RCMP in Squamish. Tell them Barney O'Malley had bought the farm. He'd been shot and killed a little while ago right here on location. Also, let them know we were going to try and tail a banged-up old grey Ford Fairlane that was hellbent for the city. The driver was probably the guy who did it.

I said the Mounties should talk to a tall, good-looking woman with dark brown hair standing near the woods with the two young girls who'd found the body. She was to take them home to her place as soon as the police were finished interviewing them. And, not to worry, Dan and Leo wouldn't be taking any stupid chances.

Which turned out to be a lie.

The first dumb thing I did was to suggest taking my car instead of hunting down Bob Melts for the keys to his Ferrari, the only other vehicle outside the wall of movie rigs. The second was to be driving with a stunt man as a passenger.

It was fine at the start. Pushing the Mini as fast as I could, I filled Leo in on recent developments and gave him some background on Georgia West and the man we were chasing, Donny Breen. "He sounds a real rang-a-tang," he remarked. Especially when Breen was all coked up, I said, as he probably was now. We'd better be careful because instead of his usual knife, he might still be carrying the gun he'd used on O'Malley.

❖❖

"Why would Breen risk coming up here to kill O'Malley?" Leo wondered.

"Maybe he and O'Malley were somehow in this together— as I'm starting to assume. And maybe O'Malley chose the meeting place. Figured they could be safely out of sight in the woods around Shannon Falls. Yet still well within earshot of the film crew if Barney needed help. Or so he thought."

We fell into silence. No sign of the Ford. It didn't take long for Leo, his head grazing the roof, to ask if this crate could get up over fifty-five. Never on a hill, I said. Fortunately, we hit a stretch with few cars and a downhill grade, so I could redeem my honour. Not for long. That guy ahead of us in the Volks was driving like a farmer with a hayrig, he said. I could get by him. I tramped on the accelerator and swung out to the left as the road began a gradual incline. We were even with the Volkswagen when the Mini started to sputter and fall behind. Leo cursed softly.

Heading down towards Britannia Beach, we had a long view of the straight expanse of highway running along the water. "Hey, lookie there, old pal," Leo hollered. "Behind that logging truck way up ahead. Looks like a grey Fairlane to me." It was a few minutes in front of us and would be a lot farther if it ever passed the fully loaded truck. Which it did, within seconds. Well, Leo said, at least we knew it was within spitting distance, if we had a clear shot and a big wind behind us.

We gained on the logging truck as it climbed the hill out of Britannia Beach. "Go for it, Dan!" I floored the Mini, which hiccuped and gradually gathered enough speed to draw up behind the big rig. I moved out into the passing lane. But we were near the crest of the hill, where the road narrowed to two lanes from three. The damn car had no more guts to give. I'd been here before, driving with Bob Melts. I was neck and neck with the truck. The passing lane had disappeared. No way to see what was coming the opposite way.

"Holy flying cowcrap!" Leo yelped.

This time it wasn't a bus brimming with tourists. Only a car with an old couple, tootling along. Headed straight at us, dead centre in the same lane.

"Hit the brakes!"

I slammed them on. The logging truck had just inched ahead of me. The Mini fishtailed. I pumped the gas. Yanked the steering wheel to the right. We went flying on to the gravel shoulder. I corrected the wheel to the left—a second before the car was about to catapult off the edge of the road into the trees below.

The Sunday drivers in the other car mosied along in the other direction as if nothing had happened.

"Damn, and I thought you couldn't hit a bull in the arse with a scoop shovel," Leo said after we'd sat in lengthy silence. "Nice wheel work."

The next five minutes proceeded at a more genteel pace, with no passing, and no words exchanged between us. Then, starting down a steep hill, we saw a string of vehicles stopped ahead of us, the logging truck at the end of the line. As we drew closer, we saw why.

All the days of rain had loosened the cliff-face at a squeeze in the road. Rocks—stones, boulders, chunks of the mountain-side half the size of my car—rose in a shoulder-high heap across both lanes. The highway was impassable.

Pulling up, we got out and began walking down the line of trucks and cars. There, near the front, only a few hundred feet from the mess of rocks, was the grey Ford Fairlane.

It was empty.

A clump of people huddled a respectful distance away from the rockpile, talking loudly, waving arms, staring up at the cliffs around them. No one with red hair, a stumpy torso. No Breen.

We walked back to the first of three vehicles sitting behind the Fairlane. I motioned to the driver, a man in a baseball cap, to roll down the window. Nope, he hadn't seen anybody come

186

out of that car. Nor had the man looking vainly at a road map in his van. Nobody was at the wheel of the car directly back of the Fairlane. A middle-aged woman in the passenger seat peered at us warily before lowering her window halfway. Oh yes, she'd seen a fellow leave the Ford just after her husband went to look at the slide. She'd thought the man would be going there too. But, funny thing, he just strolled off, over there to the left—where that path climbs up the cliff—and hadn't come down since. Why, that must have been five or ten minutes ago.

The police should be coming any minute to help clear the road, I told the woman. When they came, it was vital—it was a life-and-death matter—that she tell them we'd gone up after that man. He was a suspect in a murder that had just happened at Shannon Falls. And he was probably armed. I made her repeat everything, especially the part about life and death.

"Do you really think you should be doing this?" she asked timorously.

Leo and I looked at one another, the same question hovering between us. "We're just following him from a distance, Ma'am, to make sure he doesn't disappear entirely," Leo said. "Don't worry. We don't intend to be dead heroes."

The trail led up the cliff along a creek, probably a trickle in summer, now swollen with the spring run-off. The path was sharp at first, scrabbly with loose stones that tested Leo's cowboy boots and my Timberlands. I slid back once, shredding my left palm on the gravel. Leo reached down from the safety of a ledge and pulled me up over the bad patch. More rocks tumbled behind us. The whole area was a landslide waiting to happen.

After ten minutes of climbing, we came to a slight clearing where the roaring creek widened and the bluff gentled out to a hill. The stands of scrubby Douglas firs were thick, with just room enough along the water to manoeuvre. Unless Breen was desperate enough to scale the steeper, more treacherous slopes on either side, he would have continued up beside the watercourse.

Despite the evergreen shade, we were both sweating. I was panting, and too intent on the next step to appreciate the pink and white flowers of the bunchberries and miner's lettuce that speckled the ground. The only instant botany lesson I gave Leo was to be wary of that pretty shrub with the big maplelike leaves—which hid the spiny, painful stems of the devil's club.

At one point, the crude track we were following ended in the barricade of a sheer rockface. We had to cross the creek to reach an opening in the woods on the other bank. It was more like a small river here, raging over and around boulders that had to be our stepping stones. I went first, warily, balancing from rock to rock, managing to slosh only one shoe in the icy water. Leo was moving more quickly when suddenly his slick boots failed him, his legs gave way and he plunged bottom first into the stream. I saw him wince as I waded hip-high into the swirling water and helped him to his feet.

"Rotten legs, they're the first to go," he said as we sat on the bank, drying. He was rubbing his right ankle, shaking his head. "All the damn gags that have you jumping too far, too hard."

The wetness and exhaustion were discouraging me. My bloodied hand ached. "I wonder if Breen is anywhere near. He could have branched off anyplace, if he really wanted to hide out. Are you steady enough to keep hiking?"

Oh, hell yeah, he could go on. If we didn't see any sign of Breen in the next ten or fifteen minutes, we could head back down and send the police up here with a chopper.

He was limping in front of me as we slogged through a swampy level stretch, where the occasional alder and willow competed under a canopy of fir and hemlock. Sunlight broke through the low trees ahead of us. A couple of minutes' walking brought us to an open space not quite the width of a residential street. It was an old logging road, stretching up a hill. No evidence that the rough trail we were on would continue. We began ascending the rise, the road an easier corridor through second-growth trees and scruffy bushes. But the climb was still strenuous for a city slob. How the hell was Breen managing this? If he was.

I had just convinced myself we were on a fool's safari when Leo paused and waved me to a stop. "Up there, in that buck brush. Something black," he whispered. "Not moving."

We waited, watching the dark patch for signs of life. When nothing stirred, Leo led us measuredly to it. A black cotton jacket. Made for a big man. It was still damp with sweat.

Time to be even more quiet, careful. Hugging the trees on one side of the road. Moving slowly, raising and lowering our feet as if we were mincing through a mine field. Watching everywhere, ahead, behind, into the woods. Eventually the road had switched back and now, to our left, it dropped straight off into a deep, rock-strewn valley. The cliff was too perpendicular and crumbly to even consider climbing down. On the right, we were approaching a spot where a slide had sheared every tree and shrub and transplanted them in the ravine far below. The barren land rose at a forty-five-degree angle to a ragged ridge, the source of the rocks that had clear-cut the landscape.

It was a clean shot from the nearby ridge to the road. The sound exploded with a cannon's thunderclap in the forest stillness. Something thunked into a tree to our left.

"Dive!" Leo yelled.

We hit the dirt-and-twig deck like a couple of synchronized swimmers. I copied Leo's roll into the underbrush in the middle of the road, collecting a flock of souvenir scratches to my face. We were in a copse of fireweed, no higher than our heads.

Relieved as I was with the ensuing silence, I soon became edgy. "We can't just lie here like a pair of garter snakes," I hissed. "Why don't we crawl backwards until we're out of his line of fire?"

"Because we could be dead snakes. There're no weeds behind us for cover. We can only go forward." For a moment, Leo fell silent. Then: "You ever see *Battlefront*? Where Cowan plays a sergeant trying to take a ridge from the Germans?"

"Yeah," I said curtly, figuring he was trying to pass the time with small talk.

"It's the corniest trick in the book, but maybe it'll work. The weeds in front are tall enough for us to crawl through . . . until the trees start again and we're out of his sights. Once we're clear, we can duck into the forest and head up to the ridge."

"Then what?"

"Then that's where we do *Battlefront II*." He described the action, listened while I refused to follow his script, and asked me for my better idea.

We began wriggling forward. The movement must have stirred the fireweed. Another shot growled too low overhead. We wriggled faster, but even so, it seemed to take a lifetime. Or what little I had left of it. Leo stopped, lifted his head to check our progress. This bullet slammed into the dirt between us. We weren't into the woods yet.

Now we moved more like slugs. Noses just skimming the black earth. Waiting for another missile, which might not miss. At last, Leo decided we couldn't be seen from the ridge. The wildwood, with all its glorious density, beckoned. "Now!" I sprang up an instant later, my slug skin shed, and ran with all the speed of a startled buck.

We were deep into the forest before daring to stop. A quick catching of breath, then we walked on hurriedly, moving relentlessly through the underbrush as though our arms were machetes. Making a wide circle, we were still far enough from the ridge to be reckless about any noise. Finally a hole through the foliage revealed the first hint of that spine of stone. We were coming at it from the side, only slightly below the point where Breen was most likely to be lying in wait with his gun.

❖❖

"Here," Leo murmured, looking around at a mound of rocks at our feet. We were crouched near the edge of the woods, atop a small hill that slanted down into the slide area. Well within throwing distance of the ridge. We checked our watches and he held up five fingers. Give him five minutes. His last act was to hold out his hand to me. It took a moment to realize he wanted me to shake it. He mouthed a "Good luck" and slipped silently up an incline that would take him through the cover of trees and around the back of the ridge.

The first stage of my mission was to hurl well-placed rocks to create a diversion, like the one Leo had done the gags for in *Battlefront*. That picture was the usual paean to American military prowess in the Second World War. Maybe if I was really effective, I could act as an artillery barrage, softening Breen up like the Canadians did at the Battle of Vimy Ridge in the First. And if I failed, maybe I could get my silly head blown off.

The fifth minute came fast. I'd already picked the first stone and the spot where it should land. To confuse Breen, and while I still could stand up and make a long throw, the initial bombardment would be aimed at the far side of the clear-cut. I rose, inch by inch, to my full height and heaved the grape-fruit-sized projectile over the sheltering trees. Ducking back, I saw it touch down on the fringe of the forest opposite me. Saw a carrot-coloured head flick up over a crest of rock. Heard the pop of the gun. And thanked my father for those two summers he'd spent teaching me how to toss a baseball.

Wait one minute, as planned. Now to unsettle the bastard, a salvo of two or three sharp pieces of shale directly on target. He'd still be expecting an attack from the other woods. The rain of stones should distract Breen just long enough for Leo to clobber him from behind with a rock. It was the only plan we had.

I stood again, hidden behind a fat Douglas fir. This time, to make sure I hit the bull's-eye, I had to stand closer to the verge of the stony hill. But it was only as I let fly that I realized my feet were too damn close to the edge. I went flying too, slipping down the slope, scrabbling hard to pull myself up.

One bullet winged by me. Frozen, I waited for the next. When it didn't come, I looked up at the ridge and saw Breen face down on its rim and Leo all over his back. While I watched, a revolver slipped from a hand and slid down the rocks towards me, well out of anyone's reach. It had worked—so far.

Forget the self-congratulation. Both palms were bleeding by the time I forced myself back up the hill. Feeling no pain— anything less than a bullet wound was a blessing—I retraced the route Leo had navigated to the ridge. It was an obvious trail, thank Mother Nature, and it took only a couple of minutes to reach the summit and come upon the final scene.

This wasn't how we'd planned it. Leo, forced up against a rockface at the lip of the ridge, and weaponless. Breen, advancing on him with a hunting knife in hand. Breen's back was to me. Leo was too focussed on the knife to notice me standing on a ledge above them both.

Breen had just lunged when I screamed, *"Doublecross!"*

Leo's head snapped up to see where I was. But at the same time his instinct kicked in and his right leg, his punter's leg, lifted towards the knife—just like in the movie. It didn't make it all the way. His leg, his stunt man's leg, had taken too much punishment to react the way it had when he was a young football player.

Breen still held the knife. Yet he seemed so spooked by the one-two punch of the scream and the kick that he didn't know which way to turn. When he did wheel towards me, I jumped from my ledge. Expecting me up around his neck, he raised his lumberjack arms to ward me off. Instead I surprised him by diving to the ground and hurling myself at his feet in a shoestring tackle. He toppled and his fat head smacked the rocks with a sickening, satisfying crunch. Not like in the movies.

20

Frogs

❖❖

The helicopter descended, blades slowing, sounding for all the world like a car with a flat tire slapping the pavement. It landed on a roughly level stretch of the ridge. The pair of Mounties who piled out, guns in hand, found three men lying around like felled trees. Only one of us was feeling no pain. I was holding a crumpled Kleenex to my chin, bloodied in the diving tackle. Leo was resting up against a rock, nursing his wrenched leg. Breen was still sprawled out cold on his back, his hands and feet hog-tied with our belts.

Sorting out the situation took at least twenty minutes. They had to run through our IDs, which led to the question of why I was carrying a second driver's licence that identified me as Dr. Don Rutrick. Eventually it dawned on them, with barely contained delight, that they might have the killer of a hooker named Georgia West and the guy just shot over at Shannon Falls. And hey, maybe of that movie star, Bobbi Flynn.

Moving the suspected killer, now comatose, would require another chopper with a stretcher. Waiting, the sergeant in charge explained that the timid woman in the car had accurately delivered our message to the Mounties responding to the rockslide. As we flew back to Vancouver, I noticed one lane of the highway was now open and my Mini was perched forlornly on the side of the road.

Landing on a waterfront pad downtown, Leo and I were whisked to RCMP headquarters to be greeted by a roomful of senior Mounties and a spiffily dressed, cigar-wielding inspector from the city force. Seeing me, Phil Rusk simply shook his head.

They refused to let me call Nadia and the girls until we'd recounted our adventure several times and signed exhaustive statements. Rusk was especially probing about what had made me suspect Barney O'Malley was a transsexual.

"Well," I asked him, in one of the few questions they allowed me, "*was* he?"

"In fact, no," Rusk replied. "Not according to the coroner's initial verbal report, he wasn't."

"Then, if my hunch is right, you'll probably find that Donny Breen is one."

He lifted his brow in doubt. What made me think so, he wanted to know. Hearing I based it on clues in the diary—but mostly on a process of elimination—he lost interest in that line of questioning. Dismissing me, he said, "And if not Breen, then who next? Peter Cowan?"

Finally, Rusk gleaned the agreement of all the Mountie interrogators to release Leo and me. He followed up with an almost solicitous warning that I should stop taking mindless risks.

"Case closed, Inspector?" I asked.

"It certainly seems so. We don't have the motivation for any of it, but that will come when and if Breen wakes up. He

194

suffered a severe concussion, and they're monitoring him as we speak." As I was leaving, he told me one of his men had already called my home to assure everyone I was fine. Oh, and he'd changed his mind about having my licence lifted for conning my way into the mental hospital to see Burt Gold.

Leo leaned on a crutch the Mounties had given him and grabbed me in half a bear hug. "Now, you listen to what that lawman said, Dan. Stop hanging out with a bunged-up, one-legged, sad-assed old stunt man." We vowed to have a drink together soon.

A waiting cab took me home to Nadia and the kids. "Dad! Dad! You got the bad guy! Are you all right? What happened to your chin? Your hand's all yucky. Did he have a gun?" Nadia held back until the torrent of questions and comments ebbed. Then she put one hand on my shoulder and one long arm around my waist and buried her face in my neck. When she lifted her head and stared down at me, her dark eyes were damp. She kissed me gently on my head wound.

That outpouring of emotion had a half-life of maybe thirty seconds. The next moment, she was all business once more. "I got the bare details of the chase and struggle from our guy on the police beat, Dan. We're going to have to sit down and write the story for Monday's paper. Maybe I can call Leo and have him tell it from his side—what he was thinking, that sort of stuff—and incorporate it in your first-person account. Then—"

"Whoa, Nadge. I'm a bit cut up and bruised, desperately tired, somewhat famished, very desirous of strong drink—and I want to talk to my kids."

"We can all sit in the kitchen and listen to your story while I whip up some eggs and salad. I want to hear it in broad outline anyway so I can help you shape the article."

Which is what we did, of course. For once, I had the girls eating out of my hand as I devoured a canned-shrimp omelette and Caesar salad, washed down with many drams of Black Velvet. I even lit up a Craven "A", to no protest. By meal's end, I'd summoned up enough energy to consider aloud the next step.

"Next step? We have to write the stories by early Sunday evening so the city editor can plan a good spread," Nadia said.

"There are a couple of stories that don't have an ending. Yet."

She froze in the act of placing plates in the dishwasher. "Which ones?" The lady didn't like being upstaged in her own field.

"One of them requires a quick phone call to Rusk—and that may end it. Be right back. Meanwhile, kids, time to start thinking of hitting the sack."

With the whines in my wake, I retreated to the calm of my bedroom phone and, almost immediately, reached a scratchy-voiced Phil Rusk. He'd already heard from the hospital. He was right, I was wrong. My next call, to Bob Melts at his hotel, was one I didn't want to make. He would demand all the details about the day, which I managed to tell him in truncated form. But he was also the most obvious person to give me the two phone numbers and addresses I needed. "Be careful, old man," he cautioned. I called the first number and, as Melts had suggested, there was no answer.

A third number I knew by heart. "Dad, can you come over here and look after the girls? This time they'll tell *you* a bed-time story that's almost as good as all those Louis L'Amour yarns you read. Oh, and can I borrow your car?" Well, if he could bring one of his fishing buddies over with him.

Nadia was surprised by my theory, and nettled by what I wanted to do about it. "If that's what you believe, isn't this a good time to call in Phil Rusk?"

"And tell him what? That I have a hunch? A weak hunch I can't back up with a single strong fact? I can't convince anyone else. But now that Barney's dead and Breen is out of reach, I have a powerful feeling there's one or perhaps two places that might hold some final answers. You know what *my father* always says"—I loved this moment—"If there's a marsh, there'll be frogs. And I bet the place I'm heading will be a swampy mess."

"*You're* heading?"

"I don't want to break in an amateur in the field of break-ins, Ms Kulich."

"And you're on the *Sun* payroll and it's my responsibility to make sure you don't break the law."

"How about bending it, then—a few degrees?"

"In some ways, Dan, you're the most moral man I know. Other times, morality is like a song you once knew, but you've forgotten some of the words. So you make them up as you go along. Though they sound fine, they're not quite right."

She knew me too well. But there was no time for a philosophical argument I would lose anyway. "Have you *never* dissembled or outright lied to a source? To get a story you felt was important for the public to know?"

"Here's your Dad. We'll take my car."

"We'll have to, since mine is still sitting on the Squamish Highway."

"If you're lucky, a blind man may steal it."

I ran down to the basement to pick up some tools of my trade. Nadia drove us quickly through the twilight, across Lions Gate and on to the Upper Levels. Complaining all the while, warning me that we couldn't do anything *too* illegal. I grunted reassuring replies, my mind preoccupied with putting all the pieces together and anticipating what if anything we were about to find.

Her insistent voice finally pierced my thoughts. "What are you looking for—if you can even get in? Documents? Chequebooks? Letters?"

"All of those. Nadge, I'm acting on a hunch. Women dress it up and call it intuition."

"Yes, and men dress us down for believing in it."

❖❖

"Not this one."

Cutting off the highway, we wended our way up corkscrewing residential streets to the first scheduled stop. The house was secreted behind a high cedar-plank fence. A parking spot, carved out of the rocks above the place, held no car. Nadia parked farther along the road. I pulled on a pair of garden gloves and grabbed the rest of the tools. The gate led us into a cobblestone path flanked by tall spruce, then over a bridge. A slender creek ran to a cliff, which the brown box of a house overhung, sitting on tenuous-looking stilts. It was dark inside.

From down below on the highway, on the day I'd been driving with Bob Melts, I saw what might have been glass patio doors on the back balcony looking out over the sea and city. In the front yard, where Nadia and I now stood, a small deck had its own set of these burglar-beckoning doors. First I tried the main wooden entrance to the house. You don't know how many people leave their front doors open. It was locked. With any luck, the doors on the deck wouldn't have safety bolts securing them inside at the bottom.

On our way over, Nadia hadn't asked me once how we would manage to enter the house. Clambering over the railing of the front deck, I heard her voice call after me faintly. "Dan, you're not going to break anything?"

No break, just enter. "Come and give me a hand. Or two." I had a pair of those suction-cup clamps with handles that glaziers use to haul large sheets of glass. Attaching one to the patio door like a giant snail, I pulled up on its handle. The door lifted a little. Slapping on the other clamp, I indicated this one was Nadia's. When we lifted together, the door cleared its track and we moved it to one side. There'd been no sign of an alarm system. I transferred the suction cups to the other side of the glass, placed the door back on its track, and locked it behind us.

I shone my pencil flashlight on my watch. "Based on what Bob Melts told me," I whispered, "we probably have about half an hour for sure. Bob overheard Graves and Cowan arranging a late dinner meeting downtown—to start an hour ago."

This room, and its closet, were barren of furniture. We moved into a hallway, past a couple of bedrooms and a bathroom, and stepped down to an open space with a vaulted ceiling of smooth cedar and a vast fireplace of rough stone. One wall of windows overlooked the starry lights of Vancouver that studded the horizon beyond a black expanse of water. Nadia breathed a quiet "Wow." Looking down through these single-glazed windows, I could just make out a drop of several hundred feet straight down to a rocky inlet of the sea.

Co-opted by the impulsive act of helping me move the patio door, Nadia was now committed to the search. We agreed to divide the duties, her doing the lower half of the split level— the large livingroom, den and adjoining kitchen—and me the sleeping quarters. I gave her rubber gloves and a flashlight, along with some quick instructions on how to frisk a house, and went off to the master bedroom. The drawers and closets were a whole lot neater and less interesting than Barney O'Malley's, and the set of Louis Vuitton suitcases had nothing to hide. I was starting to work on the second bedroom when Nadia walked in and murmured, "You'd better come and see."

She led me to the sparsely furnished den, to an expansive rolltop desk with its bottom drawer pulled out. My flashlight showed me the lock had been broken. On the desk lay a slightly bent letter opener. "Okay, Bonnie," I said, "you and Clyde are headed straight for the joint. Life sentence. No mercy." Shushing me, Nadia pointed to an open folder on top of the drawer of files. A page torn from a school scribbler bore only three words, either crudely drawn or purposely distorted to disguise the writer:

YOUR NEXT.
UNLESS—

❖❖

"Your next what?" I said.

"Don't be an idiot. It's obviously a threat."

"From an idiot."

She lifted the paper. Below it was a photocopy of another page, with much more handwriting. I took in a deep breath and held it. This open, flowing script I recognized. Georgia's. A page ripped from her diary and copied. It sat on several more photocopied sheets, all of them in her hand. My breath hissed out. "Oh, damn." I checked my watch. No time to read the pages now. "Tuck these under my shirt in back," I told Nadia. "Then keep looking. But I think we've got a whole new angle to complicate the story. Blackmail—at least."

Adrenaline running, I returned to the second bedroom, where I found nothing of significance. The master bathroom. No gun taped inside the toilet tank, no incriminating note discarded in the wastebasket. The medicine cabinet held the usual gang of headache and cold tablets, which I dumped out of their bottles to double-check, and a can of talcum powder, which did not taste of cocaine. Bandages, bath salts, Braun shaver.

On a long ledge running below the cabinet rested an ersatz scallop shell cupping a man-sized bar of soap. A pair of real shells, sinuous and pink-centred, plucked from the bed of a warm sea. And a plain, mottled grey rock.

Which I'd seen before. In a gadget store. Pick it up. No heft. Grab it top and bottom, twist the two cleverly concealed halves apart. Inside, in the hollow core, packed in tissue, was a small bottle of blue pills. A single word scrawled on the label: "Halcion." Why was I not surprised?

"How are you doing?" Nadia walked in. "We're getting tight for time."

"Shut up." She looked at me in astonishment. "Listen. The door. Someone's coming in."

Her body had become cement.

"Don't worry," I said, sliding the rock back together and replacing it on the ledge. "We don't have to hide. We're going to confront him. Come on."

We met at the main entrance to the livingroom. Nadia and I stood waiting as he flicked on the lights. Behind him, looking like a deer framed in a jacklight, reared Peter Cowan. "You know, I could kill you both as intruders. Right on the spot," Adam Graves said as he reached inside his jacket and brought out a compact handgun. "And kiddo, this one is loaded."

❖❖

21

The Empty
Gun

❖❖

I hadn't counted on a gun.

In all my imaginings about a confrontation with Graves, I never suspected he'd have found another revolver, nor be prepared to use it. If I had, Nadia wouldn't be there with me. Time to talk.

"Well, number one: we're not intruders, Graves. We came to discuss some developments with you and found the front door open."

"I locked it behind me."

"Maybe you didn't. Or maybe somebody else got here before us. It was wide open. We'd just walked in to look around when you arrived. I'm glad you're okay." Making the words up as I went along.

"I don't believe you. But it doesn't matter. Get the hell out." He continued to hold the gun on us. And he'd been drinking. I could smell the cognac fumes at five paces.

"Nadia, go. I want to stay and talk to Graves and Cowan."

"I'm staying, too. He's not about to shoot a reporter."

"He's not about to shoot anybody, are you, Graves?" I suggested hopefully. "Get going. Please." She stayed put.

Cowan, silent until now, pleaded, "Adam, put the gun away, for God's sake. And you two, listen to the man and leave."

"You listen," I said. "I've just endured a day in which I crashed through the woods, climbed a mountain, got shot at and threatened with a knife. Now I want to know why it all happened."

"It's obvious," Graves replied. "Some crazy bastard, all coked up, goes around killing people."

"And threatening others with blackmail."

The gun jerked in his hand. "I don't know about that, friend."

It was time to test my theory. "I think you do. Look, Donny Breen's safely tucked away in hospital. Unconscious. Under guard. He can't get to you now. So why don't you level with us about everything, old girl?"

"What the hell are you talking about?" he shrieked. He moved towards me, behind the menacing little handgun, and both Nadia and I backed into the livingroom. Cowan's face reflected pure bewilderment. "Adam, control yourself."

"Shut up, you sleazy old chickenhawk."

"Graves!" The famous voice cracked.

Pull back. Maybe I could deflect Graves' anger and try out another theory at the same time. "I was wondering about that, Cowan. Were those tiny-tot skin magazines that Barney kept in his hotel room really meant for you? Was that the kind of thing you were trying to hide in your trailer the day I first came to talk to you? Is that why you were so disgustingly smarmy when you met my two daughters?"

"Are you mad, Rudnicki?" Cowan turned imploringly to Nadia. "This is all despicable slander. My lawyer—"

"Yeah," Graves interrupted, "Peter likes them young. Real young." He idly pointed the gun at a slack-mouthed Cowan, then lowered it while shrugging off his coat and draping it over a chair near the window wall. There he stood, his back to the view. "Okay, enough chit-chat, Rinicky. I lost my head. It's been a bloody long day. I thought you were mocking me. Now, beat it," he said in his best macho manner.

Nadia didn't move. Her eyes were ablaze with questions. I strolled over to a chair across from Graves and settled into it, my feet crossed, my hands clasped behind my head. A portrait of perfect relaxation. Tension churned my stomach. I could see him shifting the gun in his hand for a firmer grasp.

"I just need some answers, then I'll go. You might as well listen and tell me where I'm wrong so you don't see it splashed all over the newspaper. Let me lay out what I already know. As you said, obviously we've got a killer. Donny Breen. But I believe the late unlamented Barney O'Malley was somehow linked to Breen and at least one of the killings. Why, I don't know. What I do know is that O'Malley really had no alibi for the night of Bobbi Flynn's murder. That he then tried to turn the attention of the police to poor Burt Gold."

"How?" Graves demanded.

"By feeding him a prescription drug he knew could very well cause paranoia in high doses. Halcion. Ever hear of it?" Staring at the gun, he shook his head. "That surprises me. For someone who has investments in a pharmaceutical company, as the newspapers pointed out, you should be well up on all those exciting new drugs."

Graves' immediate response was to head across the room to a light-oak liquor cabinet. Juggling the gun from hand to hand, he poured himself a big snifter of Courvoisier and drank half of it on his way back. "Whatever O'Malley did was on his own hook," he said finally.

"Maybe." With that weapon between us, I had to balance what I really knew and what I wanted to find out—without pushing him over the edge. I went on, telling him how I'd observed the strange hold O'Malley had on people. How I'd heard he liked to learn their soft spots, then cater to them, and capitalize on their indebtedness to him. "Like you, Cowan, with your penchant for moppets." Cowan, who had barely moved through all of this, didn't bother to deny it.

"And like you, Graves." We were both staring at the gun, which by now had become an extension of him, like a prosthetic hand. His head snapped up. I looked again at the pimples on his puffy face. "Like you. What hold did O'Malley have on you that would allow him to give you orders and make you change your mind from one moment to the next? Why did you continue to employ a drunk who'd lost the respect of everybody in the cast and crew? I really didn't understand how a wreck of a human being like Barney O'Malley could control a man who was a Harvard-trained lawyer and a successful entrepreneur. Of course, there's one thing wrong with that description of you."

I looked at Nadia, who had lighted on the edge of a sofa. She nodded to me: go on. "I admit—and Nadia knows this—I missed it all the way along. Didn't truly start tumbling to it until yesterday. Oh, I saw signs from time to time that my subconscious filed away for me. There were the stories about your brief liaisons with women. And the total lack of stories about your more distant past. Then the image you presented of the tough-talking Hollywood producer. Almost to the point of parody, as someone said to me.

"Other things I'd noticed, that began to resurface and make sense after a man I know explained a few basics to me. Your acne, for a start. Strange, for a guy in his mid-forties. And—it intrigued me at the time—your delicate toilet habits. I wondered why, that day we met and shared the bathroom together, you insisted on going into the privacy of the cubicle. Why, if you were just having a quick pee, I couldn't hear the usual splashing sounds. Why you had to pull up your pants."

The skin on Graves' face was tight, his mouth pursed like a reproachful shrew's.

"But a surgeon explained it to me. It seems some people can't stand up and urinate at the same time. Something about their equipment. Especially if it's been doctored. And then, finally, everything clicked together yesterday when I heard that the only Graves who'd graduated from Harvard Law School in the Sixties was someone named Brenda."

"Christ," Cowan said.

Graves was rising, a manic look firing his small blue eyes. I held them with mine. "Don't get upset," I said, standing slowly. "I've just been trying to solve a mystery in Georgia West's diary. Where she talks about a person she identifies only as B. Someone who'd been involved with Bobbi Flynn. Someone who was a he, but not really a he. Another transsexual."

"Adam—Graves—is this true?" Cowan sputtered. "Tell him it's the most ridiculous—"

"There's nothing ridiculous about it!" Graves cried.

"No, there isn't," I said, as calmly as I could. "But it does explain how O'Malley could have kept you in his thrall. And if Breen had learned about your transsexualism from Georgia, how he might have used it to try blackmailing you. As I gather he did." I reached around my back and pulled out the sheets of paper from under my shirt. The copies of the pages from the diary and the threatening note, which I held up for Graves. "Did he begin by simply trying to expose your past? And then, when that didn't work, were you going to be Breen's next victim, after he killed Bobbi? Unless—what? Unless you gave him bags and bags of cash?"

As I babbled on, Graves was pacing up and down the room, still clutching the gun, that demented expression still alive on his face. His chest heaved as if he were hyperventilating. He started to speak several times but bit the words back. At last he said, "You idiot. All of you—you don't know anything. Yeah, Peter, I was Brenda. But Brenda doesn't exist anymore, she's dead now. Just like that precious Bobbi Flynn, that so-called sex symbol. That disgusting piece of crap. She had the goddam nerve to tell me I was a joke of a man. When she was a bloody lesbo. I was giving that sick little pig her big break. I took a chance on her —before her first picture was even out. Then she wanted to hold me up for more money. Wheedled and whined. Even threatened to quit. But she knew I would've sued her ass off. The picture looked like it'd be way over budget. There I was out beating the bushes for investors to split the risk and she wanted more money. So when Bobbi finally understood she couldn't pressure me, she came on to me, as if she really wanted me. Yeah, she could be a shit-hot actress when there was cash on the table. Or under the pillow. And you know what? I *believed* her. How's that for stupid?"

I knew what was coming. Should I let him continue, let him spew his guts? No, that was a job for Phil Rusk, in the controlled circumstances of a police interview room. Better to head off Graves now so he didn't feel backed into a corner—a corner he'd be forced to come out of with gun blazing.

"*Adam.* Enough. This is too painful for you. You don't have to justify yourself to a bunch of strangers. We all know what kind of woman Bobbi Flynn was. We'll go—"

"No!" It emerged as an animal snarl. "Sit!" Lunging, he planted the gun inches from my face. "*You're* not going anywhere. You wanted to hear all about my sex life—you'll listen. You too, nosy, snooping newspaper lady, you make sure you hear everything I say. And that will be the last thing you ever hear." He stepped away and turned his head to the window wall, his eyes going blank, staring at some remote point in the past. I tensed, ready to leap at him—just as he turned back to me.

"I never wanted to be a woman. Never wanted those flopping pieces of flesh hanging from me. That stupid slit between my legs. Like an open wound . . . I never acted like a woman. No pretty, man-pleasing talk. No snivelling. I got through Northwestern by being *better* than any man. Then Harvard snapped me up. They thought I was still that person called Brenda. They didn't know I was already getting help to become my true gender. It took only a year after I finished law school—most of the work was done. Almost." He paused. "I went to New York, where nobody knew me. And I beat every male I ever met on the only goddam battleground that matters, kiddo. Business."

Through all of this, he stared at me with a born-again fever. I kept waiting for him to turn his head away.

"... but I preferred people in show business. At first. More comfortable with them. Figured they had their own sex problems. So I started investing in the theatre. It was all right"—he shrugged—"but Hollywood is where the action is. A man's world. Wanted to produce my own picture. Show them how to do it. That's how I met Bobbi. Yeah, she was beautiful enough. Couldn't act, though, could she, Peter?" Cowan, looking stunned, said nothing. "But I knew she'd be bankable. Then she started to believe her own press clippings. Pushed me. Until she figured out another way to get at me. Pretend she had a thing for me. Yeah, I was flattered. One of the most beautiful women in the world—a sex goddess, someone every other man would have lusted after—she was finding me attractive. Stupid, stupid. She was like every other woman. She came here and play-acted, treating me as if I were a—a hunk. That's what she called me. And then, when I thought she really believed that, I let down my guard. What a fool . . . When I came out of the bathroom, and she saw it, she laughed at me. *Laughed.* She said she was glad, she hated men, and here I was, trying to be a man with that phony thing waggling between my legs. Phony . . . thing . . . waggling. She kept laughing and laughing. I told her to stop. I jumped on her and started choking her to make her stop laughing. I made her stop.

"... but her lips were still smiling up at me. A crazy smile. And her breasts were pointing at me, those pretty, perfect, desirable, *laughing* breasts. I went to the kitchen and found a carving knife. And I came back to her and slapped the smile off her face and ripped those breasts off her perfect body. I . . . "

He looked briefly out the window, then down at the gun he found in his hand. "Then Barney called. He'd been out drinking with Burt Gold. He was just calling to tell me that the situation between Gold and Bobbi was getting worse. I said we wouldn't have to worry about her anymore, pal. I told him how she'd laughed at me. He already knew all about me anyway—he was trying to help me make it better. Barney was the one who first went out and found Georgia for me. He knew I wanted to look like—be like other men. Wherever I was, I always tried to talk to the local transsexuals, see if they could tell me anything new about the operation on the . . . " His left hand moved to his groin.

"So the night Bobbi . . . died, Barney came and helped again?" I offered hesitantly, trying to get some specific answers without interrupting his flow.

His gun twitched as he flicked his head in my direction. "I could always count on him, Barney said. And he came and he cleaned . . . things up, and then he took her away . . . I thought it would be all right. Barney said he would take care of everything."

"Is that how Georgia got involved?"

"Georgia? Yeah . . . Yeah. The next day, when I was together enough to talk to someone, Barney brought her here. Before the cops came to interview me. I told Georgia I hadn't done it, I was at home going over the financials all night—but I couldn't prove it. She wanted to believe me, so I let her think her pimp Breen had done it. And I talked to her, one transsexual to another, said she could save my ass and tell the cops she was with me that night. I had ten thousand in cash ready to keep her quiet. Which she took."

Nadia, emboldened, broke in. "So why involve Burt Gold?" Her voice wavered a little.

"Barney . . . that was O'Malley's idea. He asked me to help him get some pills he'd heard about, through my connections.

210

Make the cops think some crazy scriptwriter could've done it."

"Then it started to fall apart," I said.

Graves' eyes closed in pain, remembering. Breathing fast, he looked on the verge of crumpling before us. No more questions. But he kept talking. "Yeah, then all Breen's notes came. He was going to trot her off to the cops if I didn't pay. And he sent the pages from her diary. Tying me in. She'd got me to tell her my birth name. *Brenda.*" His lips twisted. "And she called me B. in the diary and put in enough details so the cops would know who it was. Barney—oh, Barney said he'd handle it. It was blackmail but we should really give Breen the money he wanted. I didn't want the police to come sniffing around after me, he said. But I was already having trouble getting more money for the movie. I couldn't raise another million. Then Breen killed her—the bastard killed her just like . . . to make it look like . . . "

Graves gazed out the picture window that looked down the deep cliff to the rocks. "Now it will never get better. Too many people know. You. Him. The newspaper lady. It has to end. Here."

He raised the gun and, arm extended, swung it in a wall-to-wall arc that embraced the three of us. Cowan screamed something unintelligible. I jumped up and was flinging myself between the gun and Nadia. She was already halfway through a backward roll that would drop her behind the sofa.

The gun continued its sweep of the room until it pointed at the floor-to-ceiling expanse of window. It fired. Its blast rolled into the explosion of glass, great chunks that burst outward and a million slivers showering back into the room, into our hair, on to our skin.

From behind my shield of crossed arms, I saw Adam Graves running towards the dark void where the window had been. I saw his body hurled through the ragged hole. I saw him begin to fall, silently, into a forever where his imperfect flesh could never be wounded again.

22

That's a Wrap

Donny Breen revived after a few days in hospital and was originally charged with the murders of Georgia West and Barney O'Malley. In a sordid bit of plea-bargaining, the Crown agreed to drop the charge involving O'Malley if the pimp gave them all the missing details. It turned out that the publicist had introduced Georgia West to Bobbi Flynn, who was always seeking new sexual experiences. After Adam Graves killed Bobbi and bribed Georgia to be his alibi, Breen had discovered the $10,000 and beat Georgia until she confessed how she'd earned it. He then hatched his scheme to blackmail Graves—and Barney O'Malley had soon decided to take a piece of the action. Unfortunately, by then Georgia had learned that her pimp wasn't Bobbi's killer, convinced by a hooker who'd been with Breen the night in question. If Donny hadn't done it, Georgia reasoned, Graves must have. She was about to tell the police her suspicions when Breen murdered her. Which is when O'Malley panicked and demanded the meeting with Breen at Shannon Falls—where he told him they had to call the blackmail off. The last thing he told anyone.

❖❖

The Empty Gun was never finished. Bob Melts was relieved. Burt Gold was released from hospital, whole again. Peter Cowan slunk out of the city, undetected. My friend Leo, disillusioned about the hellish depths Hollywood could descend to, decided to stay in Vancouver and set up a school for local stunt people.

Donny Breen, diagnosed officially as a psychopath, got life. Nadia got a National Newspaper Award for her first-person story. I got an offer from the *Sun* to be a police reporter, which —much to my Dad's disgust—I considered only until they told me I'd have to work regular shifts. One summer morning, I also got a postcard from Jennie, promising to come back to Vancouver for a visit. On the front was an Old Master's painting of a medieval knight astride a white stallion.

For a day, I was a hero to my daughters. And for a while, all the publicity brought me a lot of routine freelance work in the security business. Then I had an invitation to be a last-minute guest lecturer on a cruise ship to Alaska, where I'd get too involved in trying to figure—

But that's another story.

❖❖

Acknowledgements

My thanks to Dr. Dale Birdsell of Calgary, a pioneer in trans-sexual operations in Canada, who helped with the medical and psychological facts; Sandra Slobogean of Vancouver and my mother, Christina Grescoe, for their advice on the Ukrainian phrases in the book (which are transliterated not to Library of Congress precepts but to their pronunciation in English); my agent, Linda McKnight, who encouraged me to develop Dan's family life, and, most of all, to my perceptive and sympathetic editor, Marilyn Sacks, who made *Flesh Wound* a better thing than it might have been. Any expertise apparent is theirs; all errors are mine.

❖❖

About the Author

Winnipeg-born Paul Grescoe is a distinguished career journalist and award-winning writer. He has been a reporter for several major newspapers in Ontario and Manitoba and an editor of national magazines, and was the founding editor of city magazines in Alberta. Coauthor of two best-selling books—*The Money Rustlers: Self-made Millionaires of the New West* and *Jimmy*, an autobiography of Jimmy Pattison—he is a corporate communications consultant in Vancouver, where he lives with his wife, Audrey, and two children. Grescoe is now at work on the second in a series of novels featuring the world's first Ukrainian-Canadian detective, Dan Rudnicki.

❖❖

Other Titles in This Series

Deadly Appearances

DOUGLAS&
McINTYRE
Fiction

Gail Bowen
Finalist for the
Books in Canada/W. H. Smith
First Novel Award

It's a hot August day at a political picnic on the Canadian prairies. Andy Boychuk, the newly elected leader of the province's opposition party, is preparing to speak. All of the key people in his life—family, friends, enemies—are waiting expectantly. He walks to the lectern, pours a glass of water, drinks and drops dead.

Joanne Kilbourn, Andy's speechwriter, is stunned, but she is no stranger to sudden death. In the hours after Andy's murder, she relives the anguish she felt years earlier when her husband was brutally killed by a complete stranger. As Joanne begins to delve into Andy Boychuk's past, she unexpectedly enters a world of concealed passions and sexual intrigue. Then someone decides to stop her.

By her own assessment, Joanne is an ordinary Canadian woman—and that is her strength. She works hard, has a wry sense of humour and leads the hectic life of a single mother. Although tough-minded enough to make her way in the cutthroat world of provincial politics, she is not by nature a risk-taker or an adventurer. But when she sees her world threatened by chaos and violence, she decides to take action.

❖❖

"In . . . Joanne Kilbourn, the protagonist of *Deadly Appearances*, Gail Bowen has created a narrator who is bright, thoughtful, wryly entertaining, and warm without being sappy." —Ann Copeland, *Books in Canada*

Also by Gail Bowen

DOUGLAS&
McINTYRE
Fiction

Murder at the Mendel

Art and murder are an unusual if all too likely combination. When artist Sally Love returns home to Saskatoon for the opening of her show at the Mendel Gallery, she is as full of surprises as ever. This time the events she sets in motion prove fateful–and fatal.

The highlight of the show is a mural depicting the private parts of Sally Love's past sexual partners. Shock. Horror. Uneasy laughter. But a motive for murder? Yet before long, two people are dead.

When Joanne Kilbourn attends the show, she and Sally resume their teenaged friendship. Joanne is swept into the maelstrom of Sally's life as controversy erupts over the show. But as threats become more menacing and personal, Joanne is drawn into investigating the web of dark intrigue woven by Sally's art world friends, former lovers and estranged relatives.

In this, her second novel featuring Joanne Kilbourn–single mother, teacher and reluctant sleuth–author Gail Bowen creates a fast-paced, entertaining mystery that mixes art and sex, revenge and greed, friendship and betrayal.